D0350503

HERO

hERO

HERO

Sept. 26, 1998

To Amanda and Anthony—
Best wishes,
S L Rottman

S. L. ROTTMAN

PEACHTREE
ATLANTA

Also by S. L. Rottman
Rough Waters

A Freestone Publication

Published by
PEACHTREE PUBLISHERS, LIMITED
494 Armour Circle NE
Atlanta, Georgia 30324

Text © 1997 by S. L. Rottman
Cover illustration © 1997 by Suzy Schultz

Book design by Loraine M. Balcsik
Composition by Dana Celentano

Manufactured in the United States of America

10 9 8 7 6 5 4 3 2

Library of Congress Cataloging-in-Publication Data

Rottman, S. L.
      Hero / S. L. Rottman.
         p. cm.
Summary: After years of abuse from his mother and neglect
from his father, ninth-grader Sean Parker is headed for trouble
when he is sent to do community service at a farm owned by an
old man who teaches Sean that he can take control of his own
life.

   ISBN 1-56145-159-2
   [1. Child abuse—Fiction. 2. Conduct of life—Fiction. 3.
   Horses—Fiction.] I. Title.
   PZ7.R7534Ho   1997
   [Fic]—dc21

                                        97-3139
                                        CIP
                                        AC

*T*hanks, Mom and Dad, for everything.

With special thanks to Art, Grandma, Laura, and Russ,
who all served as my early editors and had to work
through all the muck.

My appreciation also goes to the students at Watson
Junior High for all their inspirational support and
encouragement during the 1994–1995 school year.

—S. L. R.

"What is a hero? Can anyone tell me?"

Mrs. Walker's voice hung in the air. I studied my notes intently, searching frantically, hoping that maybe this time she wouldn't call on me.

"Sean, what do you think makes a hero?"

I sighed and sat up just a little, pretending I didn't see the expectant looks from my classmates. "He's someone brave," I said, hoping that would be enough to satisfy her. Mrs. Walker isn't bad. I mean, as far as teachers go.

She's not too old. Probably in her mid-twenties. She's funny, and she always gets pumped up for our "class discussions." The problem is that she seems to know how to rotate through the whole class and get everyone to answer at least one question every three days. That's what I've been averaging so far.

I don't like to speak up in class, and with most teachers, after the first week I might have to answer one question in a month. Most teachers are content to let the quiet types be quiet and the loud-mouth clowns or brains keep the class discussions going. Not Mrs. Walker, though. Class discussion means everybody.

"Good! Bravery is an important quality of a hero. Allyson?" She directed her attention to the other side of the room.

"But Mrs. Walker, heroes don't have to be male!" Allyson shot me a dirty look. I sank into my seat again, while the rest of the class groaned. Allyson is known to have all the answers, even for questions no one has asked.

"True, Allyson. Heroes are both male and female. What qualities do we look for in heroes? What makes a hero? Come on, let's get a good list up here!"

"Strength," from Robert.

"Smart," from Ann.

"Courageous," from Mike.

"Good. Let's put that with brave. What else? Why are heroes special?" Mrs. Walker never quit.

"They can fly," Michelle piped up.

"They can fly? Do all heroes fly?"

Michelle, as usual, was ready to dig in and fight. "Yes. Well, maybe they don't have to fly. But they need to have some sort of superpowers."

"Ummm, I don't know about that. What do you think, Stacy? Do all heroes fly or have superpowers?"

"No, but it helps."

"No, they all have superpowers," Rick chimed in.

"Can you think of a hero that doesn't fly?"

"Yeah, my dad," Sam said.

Rick groaned, "That's so lame."

"Richard." Mrs. Walker cut him off with the classic I-don't-think-that's-appropriate tone of voice. "There's absolutely no reason why someone's parent can't be a hero. So if your parent can also be a hero, what makes a hero? Who's your hero, Rick?"

"Chris Saunders."

"I'm afraid I'm not familiar with Chris." Mrs. Walker looked around, waiting for someone to speak up. An uneasy quiet fell over our class. We were all familiar with Chris; we grew up with him. But it was Mrs. Walker's first year teaching at our school. No one wanted to volunteer.

"You don't have to tell me who he is," Mrs. Walker said, responding to our silence, "but tell me *why* he's your hero. What qualities or characteristics does he have that makes him your hero?"

I lifted my eyes and got ready for Mrs. Walker's sweeping glance. It was Rick's hero; I could have left it for him to deal with, because I knew Mrs. Walker would return for him. But I was tired of it all. I was tired of her driving to school in her nice car after having a nice dinner with her nice husband and children the night before. Tired of knowing she had spent the evening in a well-heated, spacious house. Tired of seeing her wearing clothes every day that most of us would never be able to afford.

"Chris Saunders was killed last year when he got jumped. He was an Ice-Baby. We all liked him. He's a hero because he was real. He was brave. He was in the eighth grade for the second time, but he could tell you everything you needed to know. He didn't hold grudges, and he always backed his own."

I never changed the tone of my voice. I wasn't going for shock; I was just trying to let Mrs. Walker in on our lives. For the last two months she had been coming in here, teaching us things we didn't need.

Mrs. Walker didn't flinch. She turned to the blackboard and wrote "Real. Brave. Loyal. Fair." Then she added, "Strong. Smart. Superpowers(?)"

She turned back to us. "Did I fairly summarize the qualities of a hero that we've discussed so far?" A general rumbling from the class seemed to satisfy her. Just as she opened her mouth to continue talking, the bell rang. We waited. "Please read pages 89–95 for Monday. There's a good chance you'll have a quiz." We groaned. "Have a good weekend!"

As the class gathered their books and moved toward the door, she motioned me to her desk.

"Yeah?"

"Sean, I wanted to thank you for sharing your input about heroes and Chris Saunders."

I shrugged.

"I take it you were pretty close to him?"

I shrugged again.

She sighed and smiled. "Well, thank you. I hope you have a good afternoon."

I nodded and walked out. Lee was waiting for me in the hall.

"What'd she want?"

"She thanked me for sharing in class."

"Man, I can't believe you said all that!"

I shrugged as I opened my locker. "Why not? It's life. It's time she heard about it."

Lunch that day appeared to be a miserable lasagna made of dog food. So I spent my dollar twenty on a milk shake, fries, and potato chips instead. I believe in tasty and easily identified meals, not the ones the school serves.

Lunch was the only interesting part of the school day; it was the only time reality surfaced. You found out who was dating who, who had actually slept with who, who was dumping who, and, most importantly, who was going to kick whose butt. Today, rumor had it that Rick would be kicking my butt. It's always fun to find out a thing like that from other people.

As a quiet person, sometimes I've been mistaken for a wimp. I thought I had already straightened out that wrong impression last year, but apparently Rick needed a refresher course. I polished off my shake and went to find Rick.

Rick and I used to be friends. We had gone to school together since the second grade. People used to get us mixed up all the time, which was really weird, since we had stopped hanging out together in the fourth grade. I could never remember exactly what our original fight had been about; it seems to me it was about who was giving the better valentine card to Becky Marshall. But ever since then, we've only done one of two things: ignore each other or fight.

Somehow, from whatever the first fight had been about, things just continued out of control. In fifth grade, we'd get in shoving matches over our place in the lunch line. In seventh grade, we got into a few fights over calls made on the basketball court after school. We didn't have many classes together, but when we did, we each pretended the other was invisible. Once, a teacher tried to pair us up to work together. We sat at our desks for two class periods ignoring each other until the teacher finally assigned us new partners.

For a while, I remember missing his friendship. But then he started hanging out with guys I didn't like and he became a real jerk. Now I don't miss him. Now I almost feel sorry for him. He's so into his image of being tough and he uses so many drugs that he's almost not a real person anymore.

I knew where he hung out; everyone's got their spot worked out by the end of the first week of school. I also knew that he'd have all his little buddies with him. That's why the gang punks always make me sick. They can't even take a leak by themselves.

Walking into the south corner, I could feel eyes on me from all directions. I'm used to it; it happens a lot when you take advice only from yourself instead of from a group. Besides, everyone could tell I was ready to call Rick's bluff.

Robert and Bryan tried to stare me down, but I knew they weren't the issue. Rick was.

"Yo, man, you got a problem?"

"That's what I'm here to ask you," I responded. "According to everyone else, I'm supposed to get my butt kicked this afternoon. You heard about it?"

"Yeah, that's right. I not only heard that, I'm pretty sure I said that."

I held my hands out to the side. "Why wait and waste time? Let's go."

"Man, you are one uppity turd. You think you're so bad. You're nothing. I'm gonna wipe the sidewalk with your face."

"Why are you talking all this crap? Why're you waiting? You're so tough, let's see it. Let's go!"

"Man, first he's got the balls to talk about Chris, and now this," Robert said, looking at the sky and shaking his head.

"Oh, that's what got to you? And here I thought maybe you had heard about me and your sister last night..."

Rick slammed his Coke down and jumped up, eyes blazing.

I continued, "...but either way, you come see me when you've got something to say. You talk crap 'bout me, and I'll just shove it back up your butt where it belongs."

"What happens with my homies is my business, not yours to tell the teachers. And the next time you even *think* my sister's name, I'll kill you."

I told him I'd never think her name; I told him exactly which of her body parts I'd think of, and that's what finally got the fists going. I have to admit he can use his right hook fairly well. The bruise he gave me lasted a week. The security guards got there before he thought to pull his blade on me, so we were both escorted to the office.

Fights were routine for both of us, although this was the first one between us this year. I sat quietly, just waiting to listen to the lecture and then go home for three days' suspension. Rick was sitting on the other side of the secretary's desk. They never let us sit together after a fistfight. I thought that was the only smart rule our school administration enforced.

"Sean?"

I looked up into Mrs. Walker's frowning face.

"What are you doing here?"

I jerked my thumb toward where he was sitting, arguing with the secretary. "Had a fight with Rick."

She sighed and sat down next to me. "I'm sorry to hear that. Would you like to talk about it?"

"Nothing to talk about. He was talking crap. I put it back in its place. That's all."

She just watched me. She didn't say anything at all, just looked at me with these big sad eyes.

"What? It's no big deal. I just get a three-day vacation. It's happened before, and it'll happen again."

"Why?"

"What?"

"Why? Why has it happened and why do you think it will happen again?"

I stared at her. Was she serious? But I knew she was. So why didn't I have a good, quick answer? If it was such a stupid question, why couldn't I answer it?

"Sean, I have something I want to tell you. And I think I want to ask you to just listen; don't respond verbally." She paused and took a breath. "I see many things in you, Sean. I see a lot of confusion, a lot of anger, loneliness, fear, intelligence, and stubbornness. And for whatever reason, each one seems to run your life on different days. What scares me is that in the last two weeks, I've seen just the anger and stubbornness. I don't know what's going on in your life outside of my classroom right now, but if you ever need somebody to talk to, I'm in the building by seven every morning, and I stay at least until three-thirty."

I looked at her and nodded because it seemed like she needed a response of some kind. I hoped she didn't think I would actually talk to her about my life.

"You are an extremely bright person, Sean. And I know that sometimes school doesn't always seem important. But if you don't use your brains along the way, you lose touch with what you've got. I hope that you make the decision to stay with school, and stay serious about it. It's not an easy decision to make. But I truly believe that you will go far in life if you make that choice."

She was talking like I had a choice to be in school! I was only fifteen; I was stuck in school for another year. There were no choices in my life. They had already been made for me.

"So I hope you'll keep all of that in mind. You won't be in class for the next week while we're working on our hero papers. That just means you'll have to put a little more effort into it. I want you to write a paper for me, two pages, in ink, about who your hero is and why. Why do you look up to him or her? Why is she or he respected? What makes him different?" She stood up. "The paper will be due when you get back. I think you know that grades come out in two weeks. This paper is worth a hundred points, and right now you've got a C-. A good paper may bring you up to a B, but a bad one will drag you down to a D. And if you don't turn one in, you won't pass this term. And don't forget that doing daily journal entries is a part of our class this semester. Just because you won't be in class doesn't excuse you from the assignment. Your entries can be 'free' entries, about anything you want to write. Now, do you have any questions about the assignment?"

I shook my head. I had a question, but it had nothing to do with the assignment. She seemed to think I was getting suspended for a week. Didn't they tell first-year teachers anything? Three days' suspension for a fight; you only get a week if any weapons were used.

"This is a good time to start making some important decisions, Sean," she said. I didn't look up.

"Rick, Sean, come on into my office." Dr. Bushel, the assistant principal stuck his head around the door. "Oh, Mrs. Walker, excuse me. Did you need anything?"

"Oh, no," she said with a smile. "I was just chatting with Sean and letting him know about the next assignment. I'll try to talk to Rick before he leaves for the day."

Dr. Bushel closed the door behind us and sat down at his desk. "Sorry it took so long, guys, but I had to talk to your parents for a while before I called you in here."

I looked at Rick, and he was looking at me. This was as new to him as it was to me. Normally Dr. Bushel talked to us before calling our parents.

"As I told you both before, there was some new legislation passed this summer. It allows schools to expel students with chronic behavioral problems. In the first two months of this year, Rick, you've been suspended three times, and Sean twice. And that's not including what happened last year. So, we are now at step three on a five-step program for both of you. I have a behavior contract for each of you to sign. Step four is having your parents come to school with you for a week of classes. Step five is expulsion for one calendar year."

Suddenly I realized that Mrs. Walker had known this was coming. That's why she had been talking about making the choice to continue coming to school.

"Are we being suspended for a week this time?" I asked. Rick rolled his eyes at me.

"Three days hasn't gotten the message through to either of you, so we'll see if five will help. Three days of out-of-school suspension and two days of in-house. Richard, your mom will be here to pick you up in half an hour; go wait in the office for her. And make sure you come in before school tomorrow to get your makeup work from the teachers."

"Can't I just go get them now?"

"No, your teachers have other classes right now. You can come get them before school tomorrow, or you can wait till you come back for in-house. Those are your only two options."

"But Mrs. Walker has her planning period right now."

Dr. Bushel jotted down a quick note. "Give this to Ms. Jones. If she can find Mrs. Walker, and if Mrs. Walker has time, she can come talk to you in the office."

Rick left. Dr. Bushel just looked at me.

"Are you gonna make me wait here until you quit trying to get a hold of my mom, or are you gonna let me go?"

Dr. Bushel looked like he was in pain. "I've already talked to your father."

Even though I didn't want to, I felt myself tensing up all over. I hadn't even spoken to my father in the last two years. What right did this idiot have to contact him?

"Oh yeah?"

Dr. Bushel nodded. "I explained our current situation with the behavior contract. I also told him that your mother has been either unavailable or unable to assist us in your discipline for the past few months, and that that was my reason for calling him."

He watched me for a few seconds, trying to gauge my reaction. I was doing everything I could not to react, but I was breathing hard, almost like I had been running.

"Your father was very concerned. He'll be here in two hours to talk. You can wait in the detention room until then."

I couldn't believe it. My father was coming here. I couldn't even think.

I was crunched in a ball, doing everything in the world to stay invisible. If anyone had asked me at the time, I would have happily agreed to take an overdose of anything. That may sound strange, to be ready to accept death when you're not even six years old, but even then I knew it would be better than what was coming.

They were fighting again. Nothing new there. And I'm not sure I really minded their fighting. I mean, I didn't like it, but I liked it a lot better than what happened if it was a bad enough fight to make him leave. When the fights were really bad, he would leave for anywhere from three hours to three days or three weeks.

I don't know if they fought before I was five or what those fights were about, but by the time I was five, it was my father's opinion that my mother 1) needed to quit smoking, 2) needed to quit drinking, 3) needed to lose weight, 4) needed to either get a job or at least keep the house clean, and a whole bunch of other things that I can't even remember now. It was my mother's opinion, at least while my father was there, that he needed to either take the stick out of his butt or go take a flying leap.

As soon as he left, though, her story changed. Suddenly, everything was my fault. Her drinking, smoking, weight, and even her state of apathy. So if I had made her life miserable, she saw no reason not to make my life a living hell.

The last time he left, the time he didn't come back until he had the divorce papers for her to sign, I couldn't leave the house for two weeks. Even then, some of the bruises were still visible. And my pinkie finger will never straighten out now. She couldn't take me to the hospital to get it set because they'd ask questions. So she wrapped it for me a couple of days later, when she had finally calmed down. But the bump's still there.

After the divorce was final, I'd still see him every month for a while. I liked being with him a lot. But I dreaded coming home. It was like being shoved back into the dark cave of a mad grizzly. I ended up dreading my days with him, too. He never understood, always pretended not to believe me when I'd tell him about Mom.

And worst of all, he kept taking me back to her.

"Sean?"

I wrenched myself out of my memories. Ms. Jones was telling me to go back to Dr. Bushel's office.

I stopped outside the office. I couldn't go in there. My father had moved to a city an hour away two months ago. I couldn't believe how quickly he had gotten here. He must have dropped everything at work. I knew Mom still had contact with him, at least in the form of the checks he sent every month, but I hadn't seen him. Why, then, did he suddenly show up?

The door opened in front of me. Dr. Bushel looked at me in a strange way. "It's easier to be invited in if you at least knock and let us know you're out here," he said. "I was just coming to see if you were trying to skip out on us."

I wanted to make a stinging remark, but I couldn't think of anything to say. All I could think was that my father was probably sitting to the right of the door, in the chair I couldn't see.

I wondered if he looked the same. Was the black hair he had given me starting to show any gray? Were those Parker brown eyes still behind the John Lennon glasses he used to wear?

Taking a deep breath, I stepped into the room, and just like that, the moment passed and all the questions were answered.

He wasn't sitting. Instead, he was leaning against the wall with his arms crossed. The last time I had seen him, we had spent a Saturday afternoon in the park and he was wearing cut-off jeans and an old, faded T-shirt that I had given him for his birthday. Now he was in a sharp business suit that looked collected and orderly even though he had loosened his tie. The silver streaks that were starting to show at his temples only increased the calm, commanding atmosphere that had always prevented me from getting close to him.

He looked at me and I knew—the new glasses didn't hide the blank eyes well enough. He wasn't here for me. He was here only because the school had called, because he had to be.

"Okay. Daddy's here now," I said sarcastically. "Now may I go home and enjoy my vacation?"

My father didn't say anything. He just continued to look at me with those blank eyes.

"No, Sean, there are some matters we still need to discuss," Dr. Bushel said.

"Like what? I've been suspended for five days, three out, two in. And when I come back, I had better be a good boy, or Mommy and Daddy will have to come to school with me. And then, if I still want to be a bad boy, I may never have to come back to this stinking hole again. Did I miss anything?"

"What matters to you, Sean?"

"Huh?"

"I've been watching you, ever since you got here as a seventh grader. You were fine your first year. Last year, you were in trouble a lot, especially in the spring. So far this year, you seem to be planning to pick up where you left off last year. You act like you don't care about anything, but I know that can't be true. I'd like to know what matters to you."

I just looked at him. What did he think I was, stupid? Like I'm going to tell him what matters to me. Then he'd just take it away from me.

My father sighed. "I'm afraid I can't offer much help here. These problems all seem to have started when I moved."

"Oh, don't flatter yourself. You had no idea what I was doing even before you moved."

My father raised an eyebrow. He hadn't stopped looking at me since the moment my foot came through the door. But he hadn't spoken to me. He was only talking to Dr. Bushel.

"I understand the difficulty in reaching his mother. The only times I know she's still functioning are when she cashes the check. She's never home when I call, and she doesn't return calls. That, combined with Sean's behavior, makes me believe he's not getting much guidance at home."

"That's the conclusion I had come to as well," Dr. Bushel agreed. "The question that remains, then, is what to do about it."

"I'd like to help, but without her cooperation, there's not much I can do. I haven't been able to reach either of them even to arrange a short visit. This is the first time I've seen Sean since moving back to the area a couple of months ago. The last time I dropped in uninvited, she called the cops on me. I can't run that risk again. My clients wouldn't want to work with someone who has a police record, regardless of the reason."

"If I were to call—" Dr. Bushel began.

I turned around and started toward the door.

"Where do you think you're going?" a voice asked sharply. Dr. Bushel's voice, not my father's.

"Well, y'all are just talkin' about me, so I don't need to be here. I think I'll just go home."

"Sit down!" Dr. Bushel commanded.

I reached for the doorknob.

"Sean, we're not done here," Dr. Bushel said, raising his voice even more.

I stepped into the long empty hallway, and moved toward the door.

"Young man, get back here!" Dr. Bushel nearly shouted.

Halfway down the hall, I heard my father. "Sean, you're not making this any easier!"

Ha! Why should I make anything any easier for him? He could have—no, he should have—just stayed away. I didn't need him.

When I opened the door, I was blinded by the deceiving sunlight. It was cold.

chapter two

As carefully as possible, I opened the front door. I knew my mom was sleeping in the back room, but it was a small house and the front door squeaked. Waking her up would not be a pleasant thing.

I slipped down the hall into my room, not at all bothered by the fact that the entire house was dark. Mom always kept the blinds drawn since she slept days. I was not entirely sure what she did at night, but because it meant she wasn't home to interfere with my nighttime entertainment, it didn't bother me much. I shut the door to my room before I turned on the single bare bulb on the ceiling.

Kneeling by the bottom left corner of my bed, I pulled out an old sock. I groaned. It was empty. She had found it.

By the time I was eight I was hiding any cash I had, by ten I was moving it every two weeks, and by thirteen I was keeping a backup stash. It really sucked when she found one, but at least that left me half.

I went to my desk and opened my dictionary. I had my other half under *S* for slut. It's definitely the best hiding spot I've come up with. My mom would never think to look in a book—I guess I must have gotten my love of reading from my dad. But if I don't leave some in another place, she might start checking the books in desperation.

It was Friday afternoon. I had twenty-three bucks. I didn't have to go back to school till Thursday, which meant I didn't have to be any specific place for the next five days. I should have been feeling great. At least I was free for a few days.

Mike and I were walking along Highway 15 when my luck for the day went from bad to worse. At the time I didn't think my luck could get any worse.

Actually the afternoon had been okay; I just kicked back at the old canal until school got out for everyone else. Then Mike and I hooked up with a couple of chicks from another school and went to a party at someone's house with them. It was cool. A seven-dollar cover for all we could drink. I can't believe how stupid some parents are. I hope they knew when they left home there wouldn't be any liquor left in the cabinet when they got back from vacation.

I was glad we had managed to hook up with the girls. The only other party Mike and I had heard about was not a place I really wanted to be. It was being given by one of Rick's homies, and the chance of Rick not being there didn't really exist.

As it was, there was a lot of discussion about Rick at this party. When people found out (because Mike couldn't keep his fat mouth shut) that I not only knew Rick but had stood up to him successfully several times, it seemed like Rick was all they wanted to talk about.

I honestly didn't understand why Rick was so amazing to some people. As far as I could tell, he was just a stupid big-gang member wanna-be. He couldn't get in with the big gangs, so he had his own little gang that seemed to think they ran the school. I guess the big-time gang knew he was just a little pushover, like I did. What got me was the fact that no one else in our school seemed to have picked up on that. He kept trying to do things that looked mean and tough, but he was so stupid he always got caught doing them. He certainly could intimidate a lot of kids, including Mike. Maybe that was the reason why Mike seemed to hover around me at school.

With all the hype about Rick and the fight we had had that afternoon, I was bored with the party. I couldn't get the girl I wanted away from the crowd; they followed us everywhere. She didn't seem to mind it. In fact, she really enjoyed all the attention we were getting. She started flirting with all the other guys. I was getting mad and was ready to leave, but Mike was thriving on the attention too, and he wasn't ready to go.

Anyway, we stayed until about three, when I got really irritated. The chick I was trying to get with had managed to get away from the crowd with some other dude. When I saw her slip into a back room after him, I had had enough. I told Mike I was leaving, with or without him. He didn't want to walk all that way back home alone. He knew that was a real good way to get jumped.

So we left. As we crossed the field behind the house, we saw the flashing lights of cops going to bust the party. I was glad something in my life worked in my favor. It was the third time that month that I had decided to leave a place just minutes before the pigs showed. I was stupid enough to think my bad luck streak for the day was over.

We decided to head to my house; it'd be empty at least until seven, so we could catch a couple hours sleep and then take off before my mom got home.

Any other time we would have avoided the shortcut along Highway 15, but we figured so many cops would be busy busting the party that they wouldn't be patrolling the highway. We were wrong.

The pig was smart. I have to give him that much. He didn't flash the lights till he was right behind us. Even so, we gave him a pretty good run. Mike's run turned out better than mine; when we split up, the cop followed me.

Riding in the back of a patrol car was not a new experience for me. As the sergeant pointed out as he completed the paperwork for my file at the station, this was my fourth curfew violation in six months.

"Where's your mom, Sean?"

"Working."

"Where does she work?"

I shook my head and shrugged.

"You don't know?"

"I didn't know before, either. Why didn't you ask her last time?"

"You never told us this was going to become a habit."

Now that was a stupid response. I mean, last time was my third time. If they wanted to know where my mom worked, they had had the opportunity to ask her questions when she bailed me out.

"Where's your dad?"

I gave him a bored look and shook my head.

He looked bored with me, too. "Why don't you just show yourself to the detention room. You know where it is. And I can watch you just fine from here, so don't be cute."

"Now that's a scary thought," I muttered, getting up.

"What's that?" He glared at me.

I just shook my head again and shuffled toward the detention room. Yeah, you bet. I knew exactly where it was.

chapter three

I stared miserably out the van window. How had it happened so fast? Here it was, only Monday, and I was being shipped off for my community service. Man, I've got friends who put off their service for almost two months. I didn't even get two days!

The sergeant had felt free to call a judge who specializes in juvenile cases. This bleeding heart judge was more than happy to come in on a Saturday morning to deal with a pathetic case whose parents couldn't be found. And, lucky me, this judge just happened to have a good friend who ran a farm that took community service kids. Oh joy. This whole thing seemed awfully convenient; somehow it just didn't feel right. But who's gonna listen to a kid like me?

For the fourth time in a minute I let out a sigh—a big, rasping sigh designed to let the whole world know I was miserable and being screwed over, a sigh looking for some sympathy but also looking to tick off anyone who had to hear it more than once.

The cop driving the van rolled his eyes and shook his head. He wasn't giving pity or lectures on how this was my own fault. Apparently he knew I had gotten plenty of those at the station.

By the time my mom showed up at the police station at two-thirty Saturday afternoon, I had been treated to at least four different forms of the accept-responsibility-for-your-choices-in-life speech. Mom, however, wasted little time on words.

"You little scumball, this is just what I need. I don't want to see your ugly face again until Monday when they pick you up. Don't," she said, blowing smoke in my face as I started to say something. "Don't, or I'll beat you black and blue. You better keep your sorry butt in your room until you go to your community service."

Even the cops had looked a little surprised at her threats, but they didn't do anything about it. They didn't ask how I was going to get food from Saturday afternoon till Monday morning; I guess they assumed I wouldn't actually stay in my room that long.

Of course, she saved the real show for the house. I got off pretty lucky, though. She only slapped me across the face twice. One forehand swing left a nice bruise on my cheekbone; the backhand left me with a string of scratches from her rings. Then I was told that I was not to step foot out of my room until the van showed up Monday morning. I think I got off easy simply because she was so tired. Three in the afternoon, is, of course, the middle of her nighttime.

I wouldn't have stayed in my room, except I didn't have a choice. When I woke up Saturday night after my mom left for work, I discovered she had locked the door from the outside. Sunday morning she left a couple of cold pieces of pizza in my room. I guess she forgot to leave me anything Sunday night, but she did remember to unlock my door Monday morning so I could go do my community service at Carbondale Ranch.

"Here you go, kid. You'll find Mr. Hassler at the main house. I'll be back to get you at six o'clock." And my courteous police chauffeur drove off.

I took my time getting to the house. It was a really nice spread. There was a huge pasture to the west, and I could see a herd of cattle grazing in the distance. To the east of the driveway, there was a string of small buildings with pens. Some had baby cows, some had sheep, and one had three llamas.

The house was at the end of the drive, and a huge barn stood just behind it. Everything was painted red with white trim except the main house. It was white with a picket fence. The whole place would have been really hokey, but that morning it actually looked kind of, well, neat.

"If you're planning on just lazing about, it will take you the next three months to finish your community service instead of just three weeks. I only give credit for time actually spent working, not for hours just being here."

I looked up into a pair of bright blue eyes at exactly my level. The old man had white hair, not gray or silver, but white. He wasn't hunched over at the shoulders; in fact, just looking at him made me straighten up and put my shoulders back and lift my chin to meet his gaze.

"Well, boy," his voice rasped just a little, "are you going to stand there gaping and wasting time, or are you gonna give me your name?"

"Sean."

"Sean? You got a last name, Sean?"

I was already tired of the theatrical drill sergeant act. "You got my papers. Look it up."

His eyes narrowed and he took a step forward. Involuntarily, I stepped back. We were the same height and build, but he seemed bigger.

"NAME!" he barked.

Shoulders back, chin up, I barked right back, "Sean Parker!" He continued to stare. "Sir!"

I almost thought I saw his lips quiver. Instead he just nodded. "Better. C'mon. The stalls need mucking."

I stared. "What?"

He snorted in exasperation. "The stalls need the manure removed. You'll shovel it out, put it in a spreader, and then we'll spread it in the garden next week." He had started walking toward the small barns I had passed on the way in. I stayed where I was.

"Uh-uh. No way. I'm not spending the rest of the day shoveling crap."

He did an about-face and marched right back to me, stopping only when his face was three inches from mine. This time I held my ground. We locked gazes, and I promised myself I wouldn't back down first. I only hoped I looked half as furious as he did.

"Shoveling manure," he finally drawled, with more sarcasm than I had ever heard in two words in my life, "is what you'll do for two reasons. One, it's what you've been doing all your life with your lies and screwing around. And two, because it's all you're good for right now."

I still didn't drop my gaze. Neither did he. I suppose we only stayed like that for a few seconds, but it felt like hours. Just when I thought I couldn't take it anymore, he threw back his head and laughed. I thought he had gone crazy.

"Boy, with that determined look set to piss everybody off, it's amazing you ain't been killed yet. Let's go. You've already wasted fifteen minutes you're not getting credit for, and the sheep ain't gonna clean those stalls for you."

18

He turned around and started walking again. This time, I followed him.

I finished the small barn with the llamas in just an hour and a half and moved on to the barn with the baby cows. Mr. Hassler informed me that they're called calves.

Compared to the llamas, the calves almost smelled good. And they looked a lot friendlier too. I really hadn't liked the llamas, with their beady eyes and raggedy coats.

The calves had big, trusting eyes. One little black-and-white one in particular seemed intent on following me around and in general getting in my way. Finally I got tired of tripping over him. I put the shovel down, intending to pick him up and set him in another stall while I finished the one he was in.

Then I realized I had no idea how to pick up a cat, let alone a calf. I think he realized that at the same time I did, because he butted my hand with his head, looking for attention.

"I knew you were a lollygagger when I saw you waltzin' down the drive this morning. Boy, don't you know the meaning of the word work?"

I jerked upright. How dare he? I had been busting my butt in his crummy barns for three hours! I opened my mouth to explain, but before the thought even completed itself, another one took over. Who cared what he thought anyway? Let him think I was a loser, just like all the other stupid adults did. You try to reason with an adult and all they think you're doing is making excuses.

He shook his head. "C'mon, supper's on."

"Supper? Isn't it a little early for supper? Shouldn't we have lunch first?"

"I have what I call supper in the afternoons, and dinner at night." He shrugged. "You can call it what you want, but it's still food. So are you coming or are you gonna smart off some more?"

My stomach rumbled. The last thing I had eaten was that cold pizza yesterday morning. "I'm coming," I said, opening the gate.

"Ahem." He cleared his throat and stared at the shovel on the ground.

Flushing, I picked it up and leaned it against the wall.

He sighed. "Boy, around here you need to put things away when you're done with the chores or taking a break. You don't leave tools where another man or an animal could get hurt on them." He turned and took two steps toward the house before adding over his shoulder, "And you wash up good before you set yourself down at my table."

I headed toward the storeroom to put the shovel away. When I had gone with Mr. Hassler to get it in the morning, he had led me in and out of the main barn so quickly I hadn't had a chance to look around at all. This time, I walked slowly, stopping to look at the horses in their stalls.

When I was little, I was fascinated by horses. I used to dream of running away and stealing a horse and living in the mountains, just me and my horse. He was always a big black horse in my dreams, with a mane that hung down past his neck and a tail that swept the ground when he walked.

The biggest problem with that dream was that I had never touched a horse, let alone ridden one.

As I looked at the horses in the stalls, I felt a little afraid of them. Having never been next to a horse except in my dreams, I had not realized how big they really are.

There was one dark brown horse who came and stuck its head over the door and looked at me when I came by. I looked at the nameplate hanging above its head.

"Hey there, Star," I said, looking at the white mark on its forehead. Someone with a good imagination must have thought it looked like a star. Star stretched his? her? neck out pretty far and tried to sniff me. Then Star snorted. When I jumped, Star jumped too. I looked around, to see if anyone had seen me. I felt really stupid.

I reached out, trying to touch Star's forehead. The horse let me get pretty close. I was smiling, still trying to relax, when my stomach rumbled again. Star jerked his head up really fast, and I jumped away again. I decided to go put the shovel away so I could go eat.

It took me longer than I expected to put the shovel away, because when I leaned it against the wall in the storeroom, it fell over and took several other tools with it. Already I knew better than to leave the storeroom a mess, so I straightened everything up. By the time I got to the main house, I was starving. The only thing I had on my mind was shoving as much food in my face as soon as I could.

I made the mistake of going to the table without washing. It was a mistake I would never make again.

I pulled a chair back from the table, but as I went to sit in it, it was pulled out from underneath me. I landed, and landed hard, on my butt on the tile floor.

"Owww!" I hollered. "What'd you do that for?"

"Let me see your hands."

"What?"

"Not more than ten minutes ago, I told you to wash up before you sat down at my table. I didn't hear any water running in the house, so I'd like to know how you cleaned yourself up without it."

I glared at him. "Sorry," I said, in one of my better snotty voices. "I forgot. I'll go do it right now."

"Yes," Mr. Hassler said. "You will." Then he proceeded to half-drag, half-push me up to the bathroom. He immediately started to wash my hands and face for me.

"Jeez, man, I can do it myself," I said, trying to wrench away from him.

"No," he said. "Obviously you don't know how to do this, or you would have done it when I asked you to. So I'll just show you how it's done." He just kept on washing me, not seeming to notice that I was struggling.

I did my best to stop him, but he was a tough old fart. I didn't realize I had said that out loud until he "accidentally" got a lot of soap in my mouth.

"Yuck! Watch it! I told you I can do this, and a lot better than you. I won't miss and get it in my mouth!" I leaned over the sink and spit as much of the suds as I could out of my mouth.

"I didn't miss," he said, calmly continuing to scrub my face after I finished spitting. "Right now your mouth seems to be as dirty as your hands. I'm just trying to help you clean it up."

"Oh, you're real funny," I said.

He tossed me a towel and started out of the bathroom. "I'm assuming I won't have to help you again." His voice rose in a question. When I didn't respond immediately, he turned and started to take a step toward me.

"No," I said quickly. "No, sir, you won't have to do this again."

After that wonderful experience, I really didn't think I had much of an appetite left, but the food was delicious. Fried chicken, mashed potatoes, carrots and peas, lemonade, and an apple pie waiting for dessert. I hadn't eaten this well since I had spent the night at a friend's house two months ago and his mom made us dinner.

Unfortunately, the company was awkward. I didn't know what to say to the old man, and it was just the two of us. He said his ranch hand, James, was in town making a delivery and placing an order for grain. It would have been bad enough to have the two of us eating together, but to top it off, he had to sit there and just stare at me. He didn't eat anything, and he made no effort to talk either.

I still managed to stuff three pieces of chicken in my face, and two helpings of the vegetables. It wasn't easy. I hate eating when people watch me. But, man, I was hungry!

"You still got room for pie?" he asked gruffly.

I nodded. He served me a piece that looked like a quarter of the pie. "Wow. Thanks."

"You're welcome." He sat back in his chair and fished a pipe out of his shirt pocket. He stuck it in his mouth, without tobacco and without lighting it.

I must have looked at him in a strange way, because suddenly he grinned and almost looked embarrassed. "I picked this up in the war, and when I returned, the wife made me give it up. Well, I gave up smoking, but I can't seem to give up the pipe."

"Oh," I said, and felt really stupid. I racked my brain for something else to say. "What war?" I asked, and then felt even stupider.

He looked at me for a long moment before he said, "World War II."

"Oh," I said again, grasping frantically. "Were you in the air force?"

"Army."

"Oh." I nodded agreeably, but couldn't think of anything else to say, so I shoved another bite of pie in my mouth. He just watched me. It was beginning to get a little spooky.

I finished the pie and pushed my chair back so quickly I almost knocked it over. "I guess I'll get back to work." And then I couldn't help myself. "After all, I want to get as many hours of credit these next three days as I can." I tried, but I know my voice didn't make the sarcasm sound nearly as cutting as his did.

"Why aren't you in school?"

"Didn't you read my file?" I moaned.

"I know why you're here for community service," Mr. H. said flatly. "But usually community service has to be done on your own time—not while you're supposed to be in school."

"I was suspended."

"For what?"

"Fighting."

"What was this fight about?"

I gave him a bored look. "Nothing."

"Nothing? That's got to be the worst reason I've ever heard for fighting. If you're going to fight, there ought to be a reason for it."

I didn't say anything.

"How long is your suspension?"

"Three days out of school, then two days in. So if you don't mind, I'd like to get as many hours as I can between now and Wednesday night." After Wednesday, all of the hours would be coming out of my weekends and after school time. That was *my* time, and I didn't want to lose it.

"What's this 'in' you're talking about?"

"In-school suspension. I go to school, but instead of going to my classes, they put me in a separate room at a desk to do schoolwork and be bored out of my mind all day."

"You're kidding."

I shook my head.

His face crinkled up in a mixture of confusion and distaste. "What's the purpose of that?"

I shrugged. How was I supposed to know?

"Okay," he said, sighing and shaking his head. "I'll come get you for a short break at three-thirty. It will probably take you the rest of the day to finish the small barns. We'll hit the big one tomorrow."

chapter four

By the time he came to get me for my break, I was done with the cow barn. I could tell he was actually impressed with what I had accomplished. Especially since he tried so hard to find something wrong. I swear, we spent half an hour looking at the work I had done, but he couldn't find any fault with it. I mean, it's really not hard to tell if the crap's been cleaned out or not. But he sure spent a lot of time looking for something to criticize.

We started walking to the horse barn. About halfway there, he gave me a sheepish grin. "If you keep this pace up, I won't have enough work to keep you busy for your eighty hours of service. They'll have to send you some-place else to finish up."

I was considering what this information might mean to me when a guy in faded blue jeans, a beat-up red flannel shirt, and dusty cowboy boots came sprinting out of the main barn.

"Boss!" he shouted. "Manda just went into labor!"

Mr. Hassler stopped in his tracks. "Are you sure?" he bellowed. He looked pretty upset.

The cowboy nodded his head frantically.

"Go call Doc Wharton. Tell him we got an early delivery for him. C'mon, boy, we got an emergency situation for you to help with."

He started off at a pretty brisk pace for the barn.

"Huh?" I finally came up with an award-winning comment for the situation.

He didn't stop, slow down, or even respond. He was headed for the barn, and nothing was going to stop him. I jogged after him into the musty air.

"What kind of emergency are you talking about?" I asked after I caught up and kind of got my breath back.

"Delivery."

"Yeah? What's so important about a delivery?" I assumed he was talking about the delivery James had gone into town for. "Is the hay going to rot or something?"

Mr. Hassler snorted. "Boy, are you really that stupid? Didn't you hear James?"

I tried to recall exactly what James had said, but I really couldn't remember. Apparently I took too long trying to answer, because Mr. Hassler graciously filled me in.

"The delivery," he snapped off each word like a firecracker, "is coming from a mare in the form of a foal that's nearly two weeks premature."

"Huh?"

"For Pete's sake, city boy, a horse is having her baby too early!"

I stopped in my tracks. "Oh, no. Oh, no you don't. You can't even expect me to help a horse have a baby. Not after shoveling crap all day. I won't do this."

I had turned around and taken three steps back toward the house when an iron-hot pain shot down my arm. I looked down and saw an ancient hand gripping my shoulder so tightly I would have bruises the next day.

From the hand I looked up, following a wiry arm until I saw his red face with those intense eyes bulging out at me.

"If I had the time, I would tan your hide for your selfish attitude. But I don't have the time. I have two lives that are depending on you and me getting over there to help them survive. I can't do this myself. I need you. She needs you. The little guy waiting to be born needs you. How dare you disrespect life?"

Halfway through this fun speech, he began dragging me down to the fifth stall on the right, and then shoved me into it.

The horse, he had called her a mare, was on her side. She was reddish brown with a thick mane and tail. When she rolled her eyes at us, I could see the whites. She kicked her legs, trying to get up, and I saw the flash of her steel horseshoes. Mr. Hassler shoved past me and fell. At least I thought he did. Then I figured out that he had thrown himself on her to hold her head down so she would quit thrashing so much.

"Shhh, Manda. Hush, honey. It's okay," he murmured to her.

I stood there like a bump on a log, not really knowing what to do. He talked to her for a few more minutes before he remembered that I was there.

"C'mere, boy."

25

I approached slowly. Her legs had stopped kicking, but her sides were still heaving. I couldn't quite tell which was louder, her panting or the pounding of my heart.

"Come down here and hold her head. I've got to help at the other end."

I almost objected to holding her head down until I realized what was probably going to be involved at the other end. I dropped to my knees by her head and placed my hands as close to his as I could.

"Hold her at the muzzle and at the back of her head. It'll probably take all of your weight since you're so small."

Since I knew where the back of her head was, I guessed that the muzzle must be her nose. I was too overwhelmed to complain about being called small, even though it was one of my biggest pet peeves.

"Boss." We both looked up to see the cowboy, James, in the stall doorway. "Doc can't make it tonight. He's across town, and they've got two deliveries tonight. One was scheduled, the other's a preemie like ours, so his assistant is out there too."

Mr. Hassler swore. Then he gave James a list of things to fetch.

"Sorry, boy, looks like you're in this till the end. It will take all three of us to help her out." I couldn't answer because I was concentrating too much on holding her head. Sometimes she'd be fighting and it took all my weight, and other times she'd relax and I'd try to relax too, to make it a little more comfortable for her.

The next three hours were unbelievably long. I tried hard not to let what was going on at the other end involve me, but it was impossible. It turned out that because the baby horse, which they were calling the "foal," was early, it hadn't turned around the right way. So not only were we worried about the mare hurting herself or one of us, but we were also worried about the foal strangling on the umbilical cord before it had a chance to take its first breath.

I didn't mind watching too much at first, but then it got kind of bloody and gross. Even then, though, I couldn't stop looking. It was amazing, seeing this foal's early entry into the world.

Suddenly, Mr. Hassler and James both leaned back, with a slippery, bloody miniature horse on their laps. Manda's breathing started to slow down. So did mine.

The foal was exhausted. We all were. Manda relaxed her head in my lap, and it was heavy. We all sat there, no one moving, for several minutes. It felt really good. Then Manda lifted her head and began to get up.

James stood up quickly and spread his arms, keeping her from dropping her head to her foal. Mr. Hassler gathered the foal in his arms and began to carry it from the stall.

"Hey, what's going on?" I asked. "Doesn't he need his mom?"

Neither man answered me; they were both concentrating on the mare and her foal. Mr. Hassler was only two feet away from the door when the mare lunged. He turned instinctively, and she missed the foal, ripping his shirt instead. He stepped out of the door, and James shut it, dragging me out just as Manda lunged again.

"Boss, she got you," James said, and I saw the fresh blood spreading down his shirt.

He didn't even glance at his shirt, he just started down the row of stalls, entering a small one clear at the other end of the barn. It had a thick layer of straw already laid down, and there was an overturned bucket and a stack of clean cloths in the corner. Mr. Hassler set the foal down gently in the straw. Then he turned to us.

"Boy, you start helping this little guy out. Use those cloths and clean him off real well. Get him clean, but be gentle. Don't hurt him. James and me'll go settle Manda and clean her stall."

"And clean ourselves," James added.

Mr. Hassler nodded, but he really didn't stop talking. "Then we'll be back to help you feed him." He turned his back on me and left with James.

I was confused. I was angry at the way he was treating me. I was angry at the way he was treating the foal. I was tempted to just turn and leave. Who cared if I left? So I'd get more community service hours thrown at me, who cared?

But then I heard a noise in the straw. I turned and saw the foal trying to stand. He got up twice, but his wobbly legs wouldn't hold him, and he fell back down. After the second try, he quit and just lay there looking at me with these impossibly big eyes.

He was shaking and covered with disgusting bloody slime. I didn't want to be in the same stall with him, let alone touch him. But he was begging me with his eyes. He was pleading for help. And I knew how much it hurt to ask for help and be denied.

"Oh, hell," I said. "Somebody's got to help you out. And since it ain't gonna be Mr. H. or James or your mama, I guess it's gotta be me."

I picked up a cloth and began wiping him off. I talked to him the whole time, too. He was really interested. He never took his eyes off me.

chapter five

By the time Mr. H. returned, I had wiped the foal down not once, but twice. He was the softest thing I had ever held. After I wiped him down the first time, I sat down and held him in my lap. His brown eyes seemed to take up half his face. His coat was the color of a really new penny.

He started sucking on my fingers when I tried to wipe his face off the second time. It felt really funny.

"Well, boy, looks like we need to feed you. And then we need to name you. You're going to need a really good name.

"And a really big meal," I added with a laugh as he increased the intensity of suction on my fingers.

Suddenly there was a bottle floating just above my head. "Here. I bet he'll like this better than your fingers."

It took me a minute to get my fingers out of his mouth, but once I replaced them with the bottle, he was definitely excited. He started bobbing his head up and down and thumping his tail in the same rhythm. A couple of times he almost yanked the bottle clear out of my hands.

I forgot about being mad at Mr. H. until the foal finished the bottle and I looked up to see him standing in the stall, pipe in his mouth, watching me.

Before I could say anything, he said, "Good work today. You're handling him real well." He paused for a minute. "We couldn't leave him with his mama. She's a funny type. This is her fifth foal. She killed the first one before we had a chance to realize what was going on. We were a little quicker on the second one, but she still managed to slash the foal on the leg, and the scar she got will never fade. We've gotten better with the last three."

"Why? Why doesn't she want her own kids?"

He shook his head. "Some mares are funny that way. We don't know why."

"Then why let her keep having them?"

"Well," he said with a sigh, "she's got real good bloodlines in her." He pointed to the foal. We usually get good racing lines from her. Her third foal is in training for the state steeplechase right now." He leaned against the stall door. "She's real good in terms of the foals she gives us, but she just doesn't know how to take care of them."

We were quiet for a few minutes. The foal had stretched out a little and was sleeping, still half on my lap. Suddenly, my stomach grumbled loudly in the silence.

Mr. Hassler laughed. "Let's go get you some more grub, and then James'll take you on home."

"What time is it?"

"Almost eight."

"No wonder I'm starved. What happened to the cop?"

"He was waiting at the house when I went in to clean up. I told him we'd get you home. I figured since you did all that hard work with the delivery that you deserved to see what the little guy would really be like."

"Thanks," I said, as I tried to squirm out from under the foal without waking him up. I stood up, and would have fallen back down on the foal if Mr. Hassler hadn't reached out and caught me.

He grinned. "Legs asleep?" I nodded. He put an arm around me. "Well, better start walking it off."

Dinner that night was just leftovers from lunch, but I sure wasn't complaining. I think it was actually better the second time around. And this time James joined us, although it probably wouldn't have been so bad if I had been alone with Mr. Hassler. Now we had something in common to talk about.

While James was getting the truck to take me home, Mr. Hassler told me what to expect for tomorrow. "You'll start by learning the feed schedule here. Then you'll start cleaning the horse barn. It'll be busy for you, boy, but hopefully we won't have any more unscheduled deliveries."

I turned and looked him in the eye. "My name's Sean, Mr. Hassler, not boy."

He returned my gaze. "Mine's Dave, not Mr. Hassler." And he held out his hand.

It was the first time a man had offered his hand to me as an equal.

As the headlights came around the corner, he grinned. "Now that we both know who we are, I have a little homework assignment for you." I must've given him a strange look, because his grin got even bigger. "Why don't you figure out what we're going to call that little guy out in the stable?"

"Really?" I was so excited, even I could hear my voice squeak.

"Really," he said gravely. "That foal's already imprinted you for however long you decide to let him, so you might as well call him something you like."

James was waiting in the truck, but I wanted to know what he meant by "imprinted." Mr. Hassler shook his head. "Get goin' home, Sean. We can talk about it tomorrow."

I think James talked to me on the way home, but honestly I don't remember a word he said. I was exhausted. I couldn't remember ever working that hard in my life. I had been on the go since the cop had picked me up at seven, and it was nearly nine-thirty by the time I got home. Usually, I get to take a break just by hanging out and watching TV; that night all my body wanted to do was crawl into bed and wake up sometime next week.

As tired as I was, I just had too much on my mind to go to sleep. I was going to name the foal! But first I had to find out what "imprinted" meant.

According to my dictionary, the only definition Mr. Hassler could have been talking about was "a lasting impression." Apparently the foal had the impression that I was somehow connected to him.

I spent the next forty-five minutes trying to come up with a great name for him, skimming parts of my favorite novels, using my textbooks, dictionary, and, as a final inspiration, my thesaurus. I never thought that thing would ever have a practical use in my life. It turned out that it still didn't. I didn't find a single name worth using.

Finally I told myself I would just lie down and try to brainstorm a good name. Instead, I fell asleep.

Just as the cop dropped me off the next morning, I saw Mr. Hassler and some guy walking toward the horse barn. I didn't take my time getting to the barn that morning. I sprinted all the way.

By the time I caught up with them, Mr. Hassler was standing outside the foal's stall, and the other guy was inside, looking at him. I could hear the little guy making some funny noises; I thought they were whinnies.

Mr. Hassler nodded at me. "Mornin', Sean. Doc Wharton, I'd like you to meet Sean Parker. He let James and me assist him with the delivery last night."

The doctor turned and looked at me. He was holding the foal back, because he was straining to get to me. "Well, young man, nice job. You've got a fine colt here, even though he did show up to the party almost two weeks early."

I blurted out the first thing that came to mind. "I thought he was a foal."

Doc Wharton chuckled, but Mr. Hassler answered me without cracking a smile. "A foal is a baby horse, true, but a colt is a baby boy and a filly is a girl."

"Oh," I said, feeling stupid.

"So, have you come up with a name for him yet?"

I didn't say anything. The colt had broken free of the vet and was pushing his muzzle into my hand, looking for breakfast. It was the first time I had seen him standing up since I had cleaned him. He was still coppery all over, but for the first time I noticed that his front legs had matching white socks.

"Listen to him nicker to you! He's definitely taken a shine to you!" Doc Wharton exclaimed.

Knicker! The word triggered a memory. When my grandpa was still alive, I spent a lot of time with him. I think it was my parents' way of trying to get me out of the way while they tried to work things out. I didn't mind though. I loved listening to that old man. And I remembered that he sometimes would talk about wearing knickers when he was a little boy. This colt would be wearing his knickers permanently.

I turned to Mr. H., who was still watching me. "Knicker," I said. "He's wearing his knickers."

At first Mr. Hassler didn't move. Then his whole face lit up in a grin. "Knicker he is," he said, "and nicker he will until he gets his breakfast. C'mon, Sean, I'll show you how to fix it for him."

Mr. Hassler didn't stick around while I fed Knicker, and he had James show me how to feed the other horses in the barn. That project took a while, and by the time we got to the last horses, even I could tell they were getting impatient.

It wouldn't have taken so long, but James seemed to feel he had to explain everything in detail to me. He kept saying, "Boss would want you to know this" or "Being a city boy, you probably don't know this." I'm sure he thought he was being a good instructor, but I decided he kept explaining things because he liked to hear himself talk.

Once we finished and he had informed me that he'd show me what to do for the evening feeding later that afternoon, he got me started on the stalls in the main barn. I had to get all the old straw and anything in it out of the stall and then replace it with fresh straw. By now I was almost used to the smell and I didn't mind the work so much. It was actually kind of a good feeling to be able to turn around and say, "I did that."

Most of the horses were out in the fields, so I didn't have to worry about them. At the same time, though, I wished they were in the barn. I would have liked to have been able to watch them.

Star was one of the five that were still in their stalls when I came to clean. I went to his stall, and before I went in I spent enough time looking at him to discover that he was actually a she. I petted her on the forehead again, gathering my courage to actually go in the stall with her. Manda had taken a nasty chunk out of Mr. H.'s arm last night, and I was a little nervous about being in close quarters with a full-grown horse again.

Everything turned out fine, though. She just sniffed me when I came in, and then when I started shoveling, she ignored me. When I got to the second stall with a horse in it, I only hesitated a moment before going in. And by the time I got to the fifth one, I had no problem giving the horse a shove to get him to move so I could clean his stall.

James came to get me for lunch. Before going to wash up, I stopped in to check on Knicker. It was nearly driving me crazy to be in the same barn and not be able to spend time with him. Several times I almost walked down just to check on him, but I was determined not to let Mr. H. catch me "lollygagging" again. Somehow I just knew he'd show up the second I tried to take a peek at Knicker.

"Hey, Knicker, what's up?" I asked. I felt a prickling on the back of my neck when I saw him lying there in the straw. His eyes weren't bright and soft; they looked dull. "Knick? Hey, Knick." He didn't even look up when I said his name.

"Here." A bottle was shoved roughly at me. I looked at Mr. H. He was busy blowing his nose. I entered the stall and sat down, pulling Knicker's head onto my lap. He started nursing, but there wasn't much energy in it.

I looked up at Mr. H. "What's wrong with him?"

He shook his head. "Come on up to the house when he's eaten all he will. We'll talk about it over lunch."

I sat there, just talking to Knicker, trying to get him interested in lunch, for about forty-five minutes. I wanted to believe I saw a difference when I left him, but I knew that was just my hope, not reality. I trudged up to the house to wash my hands, hoping that Mr. H. could tell me how we were going to help Knicker.

Lunch once again tasted excellent, but I really didn't even notice what I was eating. Mr. H. and I talked through the whole hour.

"What's wrong with him?" I asked again.

Mr. H. sighed around his pipe, shaking his head. "We're really not sure. The doc didn't find anything physically wrong with him, so we think it may be his heart."

"But you just said there wasn't anything physically wrong with him," I began.

"Boy, don't you know that some heartaches aren't physical?"

I pushed the food around on my plate, not wanting to let Mr. H. see my eyes. "You mean," I said, trying to control my voice, "he misses his mama."

"Yeah," he said softly, "he sure does. But I'd rather he miss his mama than be hurt by her."

"Couldn't you put him with someone else's mama?"

Mr. H. shook his head. "We don't have any mares that would take him right now. They're either getting ready to have their foals in a couple of months, or they've got foals that are six months old or older. We'd need a mare who's got a brand new baby, or one that's just lost her baby. We don't have either."

It wasn't until dessert that I remembered to ask Mr. Hassler about "imprinting."

He looked surprised when I told him that I had looked it up in the dictionary. "Well," he drawled, "you're right, I did sort of mean that you'd have a lasting impression on Knicker, but I meant a little more than just that."

I waited impatiently as he served me a brownie smothered with two scoops of vanilla ice cream.

"When a young animal imprints, it means that they think the first being that they had contact with is their parent."

I choked on my brownie. "You mean Knicker thinks I'm his mama?"

Mr. H. grinned, but it was a sad grin. "I thought last night that he might have, and I was hoping this morning that he had because he was so excited to see you, but the way he is looking now, I'm not so sure."

Work that afternoon took forever. I kept going to Knicker's stall, talking to him, encouraging him. I didn't care if Mr. H. caught me or not. By the time the cop came to get me though, I knew. Mr. H. didn't tell me, but I knew. Knicker wouldn't make it through the night.

The cop dropped me off with the cheerful reminder that he would get me again tomorrow for my last full day at Carbondale Ranch. I walked inside and started toward my room.

"Just where do you think you're going?"

I stopped in the middle of the hall and turned around. I hadn't even seen my mother in the darkness of the living room, but there she was, sprawled on the couch.

"I'm going to sleep," I said, continuing down the hall.

"Get back here, mister. Now that you're working full-time, you're going to have to start pulling your weight around here. I think half of your wages is only fair."

"Mom," I said, not even turning around, "I'm not working a job, I'm doing community service. I don't get paid for it."

"Don't give me that crap!" She had come up behind me and now she spun me around to face her. "I'm so sick of your crap," she hissed.

I tried to pull back from the whiskey on her breath. "Fine, Mom, why don't you just call the cops and ask them to garnish my wages?"

Crack! She let me have one across the face and then slammed me into the wall, pinning me so I couldn't get away from her breath.

"How dare you get snotty with me?"

"How dare I? How dare you!" I cried. "How dare you steal money from me?" She slapped me again, but I was determined to finish. "I'm only a kid!

35

And I'm your kid! And you treat me like dirt!"

She really hit me hard then, and my head slammed back against the wall into a nail that was all that remained of a picture she had sold three years ago. I passed out.

When I came to, I was still in an uncomfortable pile on the floor. My mother was gone.

I got up and stumbled to my room, stopping in the doorway. My room was in shambles. She had torn it apart, looking for my cash. The room swayed; only the door frame kept me from falling over.

Images flashed through my mind. Images of my mother. Images of my mother with my father, with me, with her boyfriends. None of the images were of a smiling, friendly woman. They were all bitter, angry, tear-stained, or strung out. None of them were loving. Something inside me finally broke.

I ran out into the night. I ran to the school and walked around the parking lot in circles, trying to calm down, trying to come up with some answers. The school was halfway between my house and the ranch. I decided I might as well go there. I really didn't have anywhere else to go. As I jogged the rest of the two miles to the Carbondale Ranch, these phrases kept me going.

"I'd rather he miss his mama than be hurt by her."

"Listen to him nicker to you!"

"How dare you disrespect life?"

"I'd rather he miss his mama than be hurt by her."

chaPter six

"**I** can't believe he didn't show up this morning."
A distant voice barely filtered through the fog in my mind.
Something tickled my nose and I brushed it away.

I heard some more mumbled words, but I couldn't make out all of them. I wanted to wake up, but I also wanted to sleep forever, and I couldn't do either.

"I thought we had gotten through to him, or at least that Knicker had."

My nose kept itching, and my arm was under something heavy.

"You can't tell with these kids any more. Especially this one. When I say no one was home, I mean no one. We haven't been able to get a hold of his mom since Saturday afternoon when she picked him up at the station. In fact, one of his teachers called the station, asking about Sean. She showed more concern about him than his mother did."

I tried to burrow closer to the warm spot on my right. The blankets weren't very thick, but I was pretty comfortable. Except for my right arm. Whatever was on it was so heavy I couldn't even move it.

"Well I'll be damned," the voice said softly. It sounded a little closer this time.

"Hey, I wonder—"

"Shhh, softly. Look at those two, flopped together in the hay like a litter of puppies."

The weight lifted off my arm, but I couldn't get the weight off my eyelids. I honestly could not have opened my eyes at that moment to save my life.

"Mornin', Knicker. No need to ask if you're feeling better."

Knicker nickered and my nose itched again.

I felt Knicker leave, and all the warmth left with him. I reached up again to try to brush the straw off my face. Knicker came back and bumped my forehead with his nose.

This time my eyes flew open. The bolts of pain going from my head down my spine were unreal. I thought I was going to pass out again.

"Morning, Sean." The cop was grinning like an idiot at me.

Mr. H. wasn't grinning at all. "If you need a place to sleep, all you need to do is ask. You don't have to sneak into a stall like a common thief."

I didn't answer either of them. I was concentrating too hard on not passing out again. At the same time I was trying not to think at all, because it just made my head pound more.

"Sean, are you all right?"

I knew I was making a face. "I...I don't know. I kinda don't think I am." I blinked, trying to keep them in focus. I wasn't successful. The world went dark.

When I woke up again, I was in a strange room, lying in a strange bed, wearing strange clothes. I sat up slowly and found a large glass of water on a table next to the bed. I drank more than half of it before I noticed the small bottle of pills with my name on it. The directions said four times a day, so I took one. The clock in the room was running, but I was sure it couldn't be right, because it said two-thirty.

I waited for a while, but that got old pretty quickly. I wandered down the hall and found my way to Mr. Hassler's living room. I had only walked through it twice, and I hadn't paid much attention to what was in it. I took my time, looking at all the old stuff he had.

He didn't have much, so I figured what he did have must mean something to someone. There were four pictures of trains kind of clustered together. A few feet away a bunch of color photos of horses were tacked to the wall in a sort of collage. A couple of the pictures had ribbons by them. One of the pictures looked just like Knicker, and I wondered if it was his brother or sister.

On the opposite wall, there was an old black-and-white photo in a silver frame. There was a lady in it, standing in front of a small house. She looked happy, like she didn't have a care in the world. When I looked at the picture carefully, I realized she was standing in front of this house. It must have had some additions made to it over the years.

The only other thing on that wall was a framed collection of some sort.

Several medals and badges, a small bullet, and what looked like a piece of shrapnel were laid out on a neat piece of material and framed. The glass had a thick coating of dust on it.

"Sean, the doctor's not going to like seeing you up."

I turned around. "Why not? I'm fine."

Mr. Hassler shook his head. "No, boy, you're not. You've got a mild concussion and a nasty infection from a wound on the back of your head. Doc says we need to watch it carefully, or it might spread. That'd be bad news, as close as it is to your spine."

Rubbing the bandage on the back of my head, I remembered the rusty nail in the hallway. "Oh."

Mr. Hassler watched me. I just watched him back. After a few minutes, he said, "Go on, now, back to bed with you."

"But I've got work to do."

"We'll do it. You'll just have to get your hours later."

"I want to at least see Knicker."

"Good," he said. "I'm glad you want to go see him. But I'm afraid you'll have to wait until tomorrow."

I shook my head. "If he really thinks I'm his mama, and if I spent last night with him and don't show up today, he's going to be really confused. He needs me right now. He may not need me tomorrow."

We locked gazes. *I will not look away*, I promised myself. *I want this, and I'm going to have to be tough to get it. That means not looking away and not backing down.*

His eyes were the most unreadable pieces of blue ice I had ever seen. I really didn't think I'd be able to bluff him into it. After an eternity, though, he agreed.

"Okay, I'll give you a half hour."

I shook my head. "I need an hour at least."

"Forty-five minutes." He cut me off when I began to speak, "And you better take advantage of it now. I don't get generous like this very often."

I turned around to go out to the stables, hiding my smile.

"There's a jacket by the door that will probably fit you."

"That's okay, I don't need a jacket."

"Sean." The warning in his voice made me look at him over my shoulder. The expression on his face made me say, "Okay, okay, I'll wear it."

I had my hand on the doorknob when he said my name again. I turned back to look at him.

"Would you like to stay here tonight?"

"Yeah," I said, meeting his gaze, "I would."

"You can call your mom when you get back from feeding Knicker."

"That won't be necessary," I said, slipping out the door.

"Hey there, Knicker," I said as I entered his stall.

He got up, stepped quickly over to me, and butted me with his head. I laughed.

"Yeah, okay, I know I've been ignoring you all day. But at least I came to see you last night."

He butted me again.

"What? You want something? You don't want this bottle, do you? You don't actually want to eat and get healthy and go beat up on all the other little colts and fillies that had the sense to be born on time, do you?"

He butted me about four times during that little speech. Finally I gave in. "Okay, okay, here you go."

He was eating like he did the first night, head and tail bobbing up and down in the same rhythm.

When he finished, he blinked his eyes at me sleepily. I yawned back at him and sat down. He walked around me and then lay down right next to me, putting his head on my lap.

"Knicker, I don't think you think I'm your mama. I think you're even more confused than that. I think you think you're a puppy. You're a horse, silly, and you're not gonna be able to do this when you get big."

Knicker didn't seem to care. He closed his eyes and drifted off to sleep. After a while, I did too.

When I woke up, Knicker was butting me again. I could almost hear him say, "Hey, lazy, get up! I'm hungry!"

Someone had come in and dropped a blanket over me. They had also left me a pillow and a fresh bottle for Knicker. And they had left a can of Hawaiian Punch and my pills. It wasn't too hard to guess who it was.

I took my pill first, which wasn't easy, what with Knicker head-butting me all the time. I fed him again, folded up the blanket, and set it and the pillow on the overturned bucket outside the stall.

As soon as I stepped out of the stall, I heard whistling. I went over to the next stall. Mr. Hassler was there, sitting on a stack of two bales of hay, polishing a saddle.

He didn't even look up.

"Go on and wash up. James'll be done fixing dinner in a few minutes." Then he did look up, with a grin that lit up his whole face. "I thought I was going to have to come wake you, Sleeping Beauty."

I grinned back. "Nah, Knicker was too hungry to let that happen."

He nodded. "He's looking better. I think he'll be all right now. You don't need to sleep with him tonight. You'll do better in a real bed."

"You been here long?" I asked casually.

"Oh, about an hour," he answered, just as casually. "Long enough to know you snore pretty loud. I'm surprised Knicker didn't kick you out of his stall."

I laughed and started out of the barn.

"Oh, Sean," he continued. I turned back. "I'm not going to make you tell me what's going on, but I can't let you stay here without you calling your mom. That's a real good way for me to get into trouble."

I couldn't see his face because he was still in the other stall, but I could tell that even though he sounded uncomfortable saying it, he meant it. "Okay," I said, "I'll give her a call after supper."

"Good 'nough. Thank you."

I left the barn and Knicker's nickering, and headed up to the well-lit house to wash my hands.

Dinner was relaxed and easy. We talked about the work of the day (James gave me grief because I hadn't done any of it) and the work to be done tomorrow (Mr. H. promised James I'd make up for it then).

"Oh, hey," I said suddenly, "I can't."

"What do you mean?" James asked.

"Today's Wednesday, right?"

"Yeah."

"Well, that means I've got to go back to school tomorrow. This sucks. They're going to stick me in a room for eight hours with nothing to do when I could be here with Knicker."

"So don't go," James said simply.

"Yeah, but then as soon as I do go back, I still have to serve my in-house suspension time. They won't excuse me from it."

"Actually, Sean, they've already excused you from it."

I turned to look at Mr. H. "What?"

He shifted in his chair. "I, uh, I called your principal this morning and had a chat with him."

"And?"

"And I asked if I could keep you here for the rest of the week, instead of having you waste time doing in-house suspension."

"And he agreed?"

"Yes."

"And I won't have to do any time in-house when I go back?"

"No."

I shook my head. "I don't get it. I have friends whose parents have called and argued, and they still made them do time in-house. They've never dropped it before. How'd you get them to drop it?"

"Well," he shifted again. "There is a catch."

"I knew it," I said, throwing my napkin down on my empty plate. "What's the catch?"

"You have to stay on the ranch until you go back to school on Monday. The only other place you can go is to your house. You need to be at one of those two locations at all times, and you must be with a parent or guardian." He paused. "Those are court orders, Sean. I talked to the judge today."

I could tell by the way he said it he was trying to warn me to take it seriously. I was thinking of something else. "Can I just stay here?"

"Sure." Before I could respond, he added quickly, "As long as your mom or dad agrees."

I bit my lip. James stood up. "I guess it's time for me to do the dishes," he said as he began to clear the table.

"I'll give James a hand. Why don't you go in the other room and try to get a hold of your parents," Mr. Hassler said, getting up.

I called my mom. Even though I knew she wouldn't be home, I let the phone ring twenty times before I hung up. I just sat there and stared at the phone for a long time. Finally I picked up the phone and dialed 411.

"City, please," the operator droned.

"Ft. Lewis."

"Name?"

"Parker, S. J. Parker."

"I show three S. J. Parkers."

"Is there one on Maple Drive?"

"One moment, please." Then a recorded voice came on the line. "The number is 468-9753."

I hung up and stared at the phone some more. I really didn't want to make the phone call. I wouldn't even have considered it, except, well, Mr. H. had worked out a deal for me. I wanted to be able to make good on it.

But if I made this phone call, it would mean that in this week I had had more contact with my father than I had had in years. What do you say to a man you never see? One that you no longer trust or respect? I didn't want to tell him about anything that had happened in the last few days, but I knew I might need to explain some of it to him. Maybe I wouldn't; maybe he wouldn't even ask. But then again, he might. After all, he had shown up at school on Friday.

I took a deep breath and dialed quickly.

"Hello."

I froze. I knew I had dialed the correct number, but this was a woman's voice. She was giggling.

"Hello?" Her giggling had slowed down. In the background, I heard a man's voice. Then the man took the phone. "Hello? Who is this? Hello?" The man's voice was harsh, demanding, angry. The man's voice was my father's.

I hung up the phone.

chapter seven

About ten minutes later, James left for his house and Mr. H. joined me in the living room.

"Any luck?"

I shook my head. "No one's home. I'll try again later. I don't think I'll be able to reach anyone until after six-thirty tomorrow morning, though. That's when my mom usually gets home."

Mr. H. frowned, but all he said was, "Well, as long as you're trying to reach them, you're doing all you can."

We sat quietly for a few minutes. Mr. H. didn't have a TV. The radio in the kitchen was still on, and I could hear it playing some old country song. Sitting there with him wasn't quite as bad as I thought it would be.

I noticed he was looking at the photo of the lady.

"Is that your wife?"

"Yes. That picture's from 1956. She died eight years ago. That's when I hired James."

"So James is just a hired hand?" For some reason I had thought maybe he was a son or nephew.

"Well, he started out as just a hired hand. Now he's picked up a lot of extra responsibilities, and instead of just working for wages, he's also become part owner of the ranch. He'll inherit the rest when I die. He's become an important friend of mine."

"You have any kids?"

Mr. H. shook his head.

Not thinking, I blurted out, "Why not?"

The question didn't seem to bother him too much. "Sometimes, things aren't meant to be, no matter how hard we try."

"Oh," I said, blushing.

We were quiet again. This time, he broke the silence.

"So, are you going to tell me how it is you ended up in my stable this morning, or are you just going to keep me in the dark?"

"Mom and I had a fight when I got home."

"I see. Is that part of the reason why you can't reach her tonight?"

"No. She's never home nights. She usually leaves at seven or eight and then comes home around seven in the morning."

"What's she do?"

"I don't know."

Mr. H. raised his eyebrows. "You don't know? I thought that by the time you got to second or third grade you started finding out about what your parents do."

"Well, I never did." I knew my voice sounded defensive, but I couldn't help it. I didn't know what my mother did, but I had my suspicions. That didn't mean I was going to share them.

"What's your dad do?"

"He's some kind of business big shot wanna-be."

"Do you know where he works?"

"No. I saw him for the first time in two years on Friday when the school called him in."

"I see. Well," he said, looking at the clock, "maybe you ought to give it just one more phone call now. And then I'll help you clean out that cut on your head."

Mom still wasn't home, and when I didn't try to call my father, Mr. H. didn't complain. I followed him up to the bathroom. He got some peroxide and a fresh bandage out of the cabinet. I put my hand up to the back of my head.

"It's a good thing you keep the back of your head shaved," Mr. H. said. "It made it easier for the doctor to figure out what was causing the problem. Of course," he considered, "having it short like this may be why it was so easy for the injury to get that bad in the first place."

I didn't say anything, just sucked in my breath and ripped the old bandage off.

"Here, lean over the sink." He poured a small amount of peroxide on my wound and then dabbed it off with some gauze. He did that three or four times. Then he spread some weird kind of goop on it and used adhesive tape to attach a fresh piece of gauze.

"So, how'd you do this?" He was rummaging in the cabinet again.

"I know you didn't do it in Knicker's stall."

"No," I agreed.

Mr. Hassler sighed. "Sean, I know it's not always easy for a youngster like you to talk to an old codger like me, but you're trusting me enough to stay the night at my house. I'm trusting you enough to let you stay here tonight. Can't you at least let me know what's gone on with you since I met you Monday morning?"

"Mr. Hassler," I began.

"Dave," he corrected.

"Dave, I can't just...I mean, I don't..." I paused and took a deep breath. "I just can't talk about it right now, okay?"

"Okay. But I really wish you would talk to me. I'd be happy to listen to you."

I didn't have any reply. I just sat down on the edge of the bathtub.

"Well, here's a toothbrush, some toothpaste, and some soap. There are towels on the racks. And there's an alarm clock on the dresser by your bed. Breakfast is served at six-thirty, so get up when you need to."

"I'll set the alarm for 6:27," I said, smiling.

Mr. H. wrinkled his nose. "I was kind of hoping you'd decide to take a shower tomorrow."

I acted insulted, and he laughed at me all the way down the hall to his room.

I changed into the large blue T-shirt I found on the bed in "my" room. As I crawled under the fluffy comforter, I tried to keep my thoughts awake, but my mind really wanted to drift off to sleep. I struggled, but the only organized thought I could come up with was that this was the safest I had ever felt; this strange house seemed to feel more like a home than anything I had ever known.

The stable had become my favorite place. I loved walking along the row of stalls and having the different horses stick their heads over their doors to see me. Some of them wanted to be petted, some of them couldn't care less for attention, but they all wanted to see who was out there.

Dark, warm colors filled the barn. The horses were brown or black; some were kind of reddish, and some were the color of a copper kettle. Piles of golden straw lay on the dusty gray floor, and the beams and walls of the old building looked like chocolate.

Knicker was up and about and very impatient about being fed when I got to his stall the next morning at seven. I didn't really mind. It felt good to be missed, even though I had only been gone for ten hours. He was so excited to see me, it took him a few minutes to get focused on the bottle.

I loved the soft feel of his fur and the way his little mane stuck straight up. His brown eyes were bright and soft, and they were always looking around, even when he was eating. If it was up to him, he'd take the bottle in his mouth and walk around so he could see everything. I knew he recognized me and he liked seeing me. I was the only one he had ever nickered to.

Every time I fed him, I spent extra time in his stall talking to him and petting him. Feeding him was the best part of the day. The only problem was leaving him. He would strain against the stall door, stretching his little neck until his nose reached over the top, and he'd nicker at me all the way out of the barn. He sounded pathetic, like he was convinced he'd never see me again.

I spent the early morning hours learning how to spread the manure in the garden. It was really disgusting, driving a truck full of crap around and dumping it in a thin layer all over.

Even though I thought it was gross, I also knew it was important for the ranch, to fertilize in the fall and to start getting the fields ready for the spring crops. Without the manure, the crops wouldn't be as good. So even though I complained about my job, I did the best I could. But I was really glad when Mr. H. came to get me around ten-thirty to give me a new job.

I didn't even consider it work after he had explained it to me. Mr. H. wanted me to spend the rest of the morning with Knicker. He gave me a halter for him, and explained that it was really important for him to learn not to fear the halter.

"Teaching a horse not to fear the halter's an important part of breaking a horse, Sean. It may even be the most important part. If a horse fears the halter, he's difficult to catch and even more difficult to bridle."

"Why would a horse fear a halter?" I asked.

"Well, it could be that the first time he was haltered it was an unpleasant experience. Or it could be that the halter rubbed him wrong and actually hurt him. There are many reasons that a horse, or any animal for that matter, learns fear. But we don't want Knicker fearing the halter. Usually we don't break foals to the halter until they're almost a year old because they just follow their mama. But Knicker doesn't have a mama to follow, so we need a way to get him to go from one place to another."

He gave me a soft red nylon halter and explained how it went on the horse. He told me to use it like a brush all over Knicker's body and to practice putting it on and taking it off. Then he turned Knicker and me loose in a small paddock for the morning.

Knicker wanted to play, but I wanted to be serious. It finally dawned on me that if he thought the halter was fun, then he wouldn't think it was something to fear. So we played.

I put the halter on him, and then we played a weird game that was kind of like tag. Then I'd take it off him again, until he came up to get me. I'd put the halter back on, and we'd play tag again.

When I got tired and ran out of breath, I'd just take the halter off and rub him with it, all over. He didn't mind at all. In fact, a couple of times I caught him dozing.

I knew he wasn't afraid of the halter, but I wasn't in any hurry to go tell Mr. H. that I'd finished the job. I'd much rather romp in a paddock with Knicker than spread manure in a field that wouldn't even respond until next spring.

Besides, my stomach was rumbling, reminding me that lunch would be served soon. No need to leave Knicker until then; I wouldn't have time to start a new job until we were done eating.

"Sean!"

I turned around with a start. There was Mrs. Walker, leaning against the paddock fence.

"Hey, Mrs. Walker," I said, walking over.

"Hey there yourself," she said, smiling. "Who's this?" Knicker had beat me to the fence and was nosing her, looking for a bottle.

"This is Knicker," I said.

"How old is he?"

"He was born Monday night."

"Gee," she said softly. "I could tell he was young, but I didn't know he was that young." She smiled at me. "You two look like you're having fun out here."

"And I've told him several times that that's not allowed," Mr. H. growled.

Mrs. Walker turned around and laughed. "How are you doing, Dave?"

"I'm fine," he said as they hugged. "I haven't seen you in quite some time. You're married now, right?"

"Yes," she said, blushing a little. "And we've got two fine boys."

"Oh, Michelle, that's fine, just fine!"

I think my chin must have hit the ground during this little exchange. "You two know each other?"

Mrs. Walker laughed again, and this time Mr. H. joined in. "Oh, yes, we know each other, all right. I spent three summers working out here for some extra cash when I was in high school."

"Oh," I said lamely. It was the only thing I could think of to say.

"How do you know Sean?" Mr. H. asked.

"Well, Sean has the dubious distinction of being one of my ninth-grade students."

"Really? What do you teach?"

"English," she and I answered together.

"So what brings you down here, Michelle?"

"Well, several things, actually."

"Okay, shoot."

"I was looking for Sean in in-house today, and Dr. Bushel told me I could find him here. So I thought I'd come down to see him, and as long as I'm here, I might as well have a chat with you and maybe pick up some goodies."

"What were you looking for?

"Oh, some potatoes, pumpkins, and do you still sell cords of wood?"

"Shore do. Can you squeeze lunch in?"

She nodded, glancing at her watch. "I've got to be back at school in forty-five minutes, so it will have to be fast."

"It's ready right now," Mr. H. said, turning and putting an arm around her shoulder. "Sean, put him back in his stall and take off his halter before you come up for lunch."

"Yessir," I mumbled.

Man, I had thought Monday's lunch was awkward! Now I was going to have to eat lunch with my English teacher. My stomach had been rumbling before, but this had made me lose my appetite.

I took my time feeding Knicker once I had him back in his stall, and I made sure I put his halter on a hook just outside his stall door before I left. Then I went straight to the bathroom to wash up before presenting myself in the kitchen.

When I was in the bathroom, I heard Mr. H. talking to Mrs. Walker. Because the heating ducts went from the bathroom to the kitchen, I could hear everything just like they were in the same room with me. I crouched down and put my ear to the vent.

"...So I took four years off to start my family, and I finally started working full-time this year."

"How do you like it?"

"Oh, I love it. Sometimes I feel guilty about leaving the two little guys with the sitter all day, but Tom's company shut down last year, and his new job isn't paying as well, so there's really no choice. At least I'm doing a job I enjoy."

"I can see you being a good teacher. You always had good hands with the foals."

Mrs. Walker laughed. "Yes, but I can't use my hands on these foals. Which is too bad, because there are times...."

I could hear Mr. H. chuckle. "I'm sure there are." He hesitated. "How is Sean doing for you?"

She sighed and I could just picture her shaking her head. "He has his moments. I know he could do really well, but...honestly I'm not sure he wants to make the choice to succeed. I'm really glad you've got him for a little while, Dave. Maybe this is the right time in his life—a time when someone like you could really make a difference. He doesn't get much guidance at home, from what I understand."

"Have you talked to him much about his home life?"

"No, he still shuts himself off from me rather quickly. I'm afraid to push with him. He's borderline in my class right now, and I guess I'd rather he stay borderline for a while longer instead of risking the push now. I'm afraid that might shut him off from me entirely. In fact, I was hoping we could get together and figure out the best way to help him, after he's spent his week here."

I felt my face getting red. They were talking about me like I was some sort of project! I wanted to go downstairs and then walk out, but I couldn't tear myself away from the vent.

"What's he like at school?"

"How do you mean?"

"Well, what's he like with the other kids? I've heard so much talk about these gangs, and I guess the way he presents himself makes me wonder...."

"Well, he's not in a gang. This is my first year at the school, but my understanding from talking to other teachers is that a gang did try to recruit him, but he resisted. According to what I've heard, there was a stretch of a few months when every time he was healthy enough to come to school, he got into a fight. A couple of times he was beaten so badly, he couldn't even come to school."

"But he never gave in, huh?" I thought I could actually hear a smile in his voice.

"No, he never did." She paused for a minute, then said in a low voice, "I'm not convinced that all of his bruises come from his peers."

Mr. Hassler let out a soft whistle. "Have you reported that?"

"No," she said soberly. "According to the other teachers, the social workers have been called before, and he always confirms his mother's story."

"What about his father?"

"Our principal said he left town a while ago. No one in the school had had any contact with him until last week. I've talked to Dr. Bushel quite a bit about Sean. He thinks Sean was shaken up when his dad actually showed up on Friday."

"Well, maybe Sean's ready to face some of the truths about his parents now. Maybe one more call to the social workers is what it will take."

"Maybe," Mrs. Walker agreed. "If I see anything else suspicious, I'll call."

"I'm tempted to call now, but I'll wait and talk to Sean. Maybe that's the best way to go."

They were suddenly quiet. I broke out in a sweat.

"Sean!"

I jumped.

"Sean!" Mr. H. shouted again. "Where is that boy? I thought I heard him come in the house ten minutes ago. Sean!"

"Coming," I called back. I almost left the bathroom without washing my hands.

I didn't want to look at either of them when I entered the room, but I knew that that would give me away. I had to act normal, even though I was fuming. How dare they sit and analyze me?

The four of us sat down to lunch, but the conversation was mainly between Mr. H. and Mrs. Walker. She had a lot to tell him about her life, a lot that I really didn't want to hear. It's easier to think of your teachers just living in the classroom. To think of them having hopes, fears, and dreams that exist outside of the school just isn't natural.

I concentrated on eating and hoped they wouldn't ask me a question or anything. I asked for another biscuit and more strawberry preserves. Then Mr. H. informed me his strawberries were the best because of his special fertilizer. He and James had a good laugh at my expense, but I acted like I didn't get the joke and just kept on eating.

About halfway through lunch, Mrs. Walker turned to me. "Sean, I brought some notes and an example of a hero paper for you to use. They're in the kitchen. Have you started your paper yet?"

"No."

"Why not?" Mr. Hassler demanded.

"I've been busy." I shrugged. "I'll get it done by Monday."

"He'll have it in, Michelle, I'll see to it."

I glared at him. "It's none of your business whether I get it done or not."

He glared back at me. "Do you use that tone of voice with your parents?"

"Of course I do. Why shouldn't I?"

"Well, you're not going to use that tone with me, ever again. When somebody looks out for you and helps you out, you treat them with kindness and respect." I looked down at my plate. "Apologize to Mrs. Walker."

"What for?"

He didn't reply. He just gave me a mean look.

I looked at Mrs. Walker. "I'd apologize to you, but since I have no idea why, it wouldn't mean anything, and there really wouldn't be any point to it."

I wasn't sure, but it looked like she was trying not to smile. "I think Dave wanted you to apologize for your tone, because by telling him it was none of his business in front of me you are saying that you don't care what I think."

"Oh...Sorry." I kept my eyes on my plate.

I let my knife and fork drop onto the plate with a clank and pushed it away from me.

There was an uncomfortable silence for a moment. Then Mr. Hassler asked, "What's this assignment?"

Mrs. Walker looked at me with something close to sympathy. "They're writing a formal paper. Minimum of two pages, in ink, single side of loose-leaf paper. They are supposed to tell about their heroes. Who are they? Why are they heroes? What makes them important? What are their physical and mental qualities?"

"Sounds like quite an assignment. Are you sure it can be done in two pages?"

She smiled. "Two pages is the minimum. I would always accept a longer paper if a student went above and beyond the call of duty." She turned to me. "Has he told you about the time he went above and beyond the call of duty?"

I shook my head.

"Well," she said, standing up, "I have to get back to class, and I'm sure Dave's got a lot of work for your enjoyment this afternoon. But before you leave this job, make him tell you the story." She gave Dave a hug and a kiss on the cheek as he opened the door for her. "It's a great story, Sean. And it might even help you write your paper."

When she got to her car, she turned around and called, "I'll have Tom pick up some more vegetables when he comes to get the wood next week."

"That'll be fine," Mr. H. called back.

As Mrs. Walker drove down the driveway, Mr. H. turned to me. "I'll go do the dishes. You can go help James unload the feed in the barn. And when that's done, go ahead and finish fertilizing the vegetable garden. We'll do the cornfield tomorrow."

chapter eight

That afternoon was full of backbreaking work. James and I unloaded twenty-five heavy bags of feed from the truck and lined them up in the feed room. Then, instead of finishing the vegetable garden, James had me help him move sixty bales of hay from the hay barn to the horse barn and another twenty bales went to the cow barn.

When I went to feed Knicker that evening, I was so tired that he almost managed to knock me over.

That evening I helped James prepare dinner. It was the first time I had ever actually helped cook a real meal. I had used a microwave plenty of times, but Mr. Hassler didn't even own one. I didn't know I was supposed to add extra flour because of the altitude, so the muffins were flat. Also, I let the beans cook a little too long, so they were a little mushy, but neither Mr. H. nor James seemed in the mood to complain.

"You've done a nice job with the foal, Sean," James said around a mouthful of potatoes. "We might want to see how Manda takes to him tomorrow."

I choked on my beans. "His mama? But you told me she doesn't want him!"

"Well, she didn't, it's true, but it might be that now she's had time, she may have changed her mind."

"Yeah, but she might not have. Why take the chance? Knicker might get hurt."

"Or he might get to have a mama who loves him. We don't know. She accepted one of the foals she rejected at birth. But the others had to be removed permanently. The only way we can find out is by trying."

"But if he's doing well without her, why mess with it?" I turned to Mr. H. "I don't mind being his mama. And he's already accepted me."

Mr. H. didn't say anything.

"He doesn't need his mama," I said desperately.

"Isn't that a decision that he and his mama should make?" Mr. H. asked softly.

I attacked my hamburger, slicing it with my knife. "I'd rather he miss his mama than be hurt by her," I muttered.

"What?" James asked.

"Nothing."

The only sound for the next few minutes was the scraping of silverware against the plates. I didn't want to think about Knicker's mother. I needed something else to think about.

"So are you going to tell me about the time you went above and beyond the call of duty?" I asked finally.

James tried to cover up a chuckle with a cough. They exchanged looks, and Mr. H. sighed heavily.

"I hope you haven't been looking forward to a spectacular story all day, Sean. It isn't as impressive as Mrs. Walker tried to make it sound."

James raised his eyebrows and shook his head.

"I don't care how impressive it is," I said slowly. "I just think I deserve to hear this story."

"Oh, really?" he countered. "And what have you done to deserve this story?"

"I've been working harder than I ever have," I said truthfully.

He smiled at me. "And I hope that's a trend that's going to continue."

I nodded, trying to look as serious and committed as I could. I was getting pretty curious about this story.

"I guess some people say I went above and beyond the call of duty one day in May of '44."

"But you don't consider it going beyond the call of duty?"

"Not really."

"Why don't you just tell the story, and let Sean judge for himself," James suggested.

Mr. H. fiddled with his pipe for so long I thought he would never answer the question. Just as I was about to say something, he finally began. "Well, it was May, but in Germany in '44 you couldn't tell it was springtime. Spring to me means life. Germany in '44 was full of anything but life. Death was all around us.

"We had been engaged in a battle with a German battalion for twelve hours when we got the orders to pull out, so the captain had us start heading back toward France. Two of my men who were involved in one of our last offensive moves decided to stay behind and draw Nazi fire while the rest of us hightailed it out of there. One of them got hit, and the other was stuck in the crossfire. I helped them get out of the line of fire."

"And you don't consider that going above and beyond the call of duty?" I asked.

"Not when they were trying to help the whole squad. They didn't have to help us. They could have turned tail and run with the rest of us, and we all would have taken equal risks getting out of there. But they knew that if somebody was willing to take a big chance, the rest of us would only have to take a small chance."

He was looking down at his plate and his voice dropped. "They didn't deserve to die there. They deserved to get home to see their wives and children. I wanted them to make it home. They were my bunkmates, my buddies."

He looked at me. "They needed help. I helped them. That's not going above and beyond the call of duty. That's merely being human."

I looked at him, and then I looked at James. James had lowered his head during this speech and was shaking his head back and forth slowly. I looked back at Mr. H., who was regarding me silently.

"Mr. Hassler," I began.

"Dave," he corrected.

"Dave, you stayed back to help the men who were supposed to create a diversion to let you get out safely, right?"

"Yes."

"Then you definitely went above and beyond the call of duty because, according to your captain, your only duty was to get your butt safely out of there."

Mr. H. looked at me for a long time.

"C'mon, James, let's get these dishes done," he said finally, pushing his chair back.

"Oh, hey, Mr. H., have a seat. I can help tonight," I said quickly.

"I'd rather help James with the dishes and have you get started on your two tasks for the evening."

"What two tasks?"

"You need to try to call your mom again. And then you need to start working on your homework. I'm sure you've got other homework in addition to your English paper, but I'd like to see you at least get the rough draft done tonight." He said it like a request, but I recognized it for what it was.

"Yessir," I said, getting up to call my mom.

While the phone was ringing, I wandered over to the medals that were in the glass frame. There were lots of them. I had no idea what most of them meant, and absolutely no concept of what rank he had achieved, but I was curious, especially after the story. I recognized the Purple Heart. I had just decided to ask Mr. H. about that when my mother answered the phone.

"Hello." Her voice was low and husky.

I was taken off guard. I hadn't expected her to answer, so I hadn't planned what I was going to say. "Mom?"

"Sean?"

"Yeah, it's me."

"What the hell do you want?" Her voice wasn't low and husky anymore.

"I, uh, I just wanted to, uh, to tell you, um, where I was…last night," I stuttered.

"Okay. So where were you?" I knew from her tone that she hadn't even known I wasn't home last night, or the night before for that matter. I shouldn't have been surprised at all.

"I was at Dave's." I would have left it at that, except I knew Dave needed me to get permission. "And I'm going to stay here for the weekend."

"Is that all you called for? You're tying up my time to tell me where you're going to be this weekend?" She didn't even know enough to realize that Dave wasn't one of my regular buddies.

"Sorry," I said shortly. "I forgot how much you cared."

"What I care about is that you've been working for the last week and still trying to freeload. For your information, buddy, the phone and lights cost money. If you plan on coming back here, you better plan on using at least part of your paycheck on our bills, if not all of it. Most of our bills are high because of you."

I slammed down the phone. It took a lot of effort not to throw the phone through the window.

I went upstairs for a while. I would rather Mr. H. think that I was actually doing what he had told me to do than to have him think I was being a baby. It took me a good half-hour to calm down. To try to get my mind off of things, I looked over the notes Mrs. Walker had given me.

The desk in the room now had a lamp, a cup full of pens and pencils, and a packet of notebook paper on it. The items, set out neatly, looked like they came out of a set for a movie about a college-prep school.

I sat down and pulled out a pencil. I started doodling, and eventually my doodling became a list of words. The list of words became a list of ideas. I had a full page when Mr. Hassler stuck his head in my door.

"Sean, it's ten o'clock. Time for lights out."

I didn't look up from my paper, I just nodded.

"Did you get a hold of your mom?"

I nodded again.

"Did she agree to your staying here?"

Another nod.

"How's the paper going?"

I shrugged. I could feel his presence in the doorway. I wanted to tell him to go away. I didn't think I could talk to him right now, not without losing it. I didn't want to lose it in front of him.

"Are you really going to make Knicker go back to his mama?" I demanded suddenly. I hadn't even known I was going to ask.

I heard Mr. H. come into the room and sit down on the bed. "Sean, sometimes we need to be able to give people a second chance. Animals are no different."

I didn't say anything.

"You know," he said gently, "it would be good for Knicker if Manda took him back."

"You know," I retorted, "it will hurt him really bad when she doesn't."

"What makes you so sure that she won't take him back?" He didn't say it smart-like. He said it like he was really interested in my opinion.

I looked at him. "Because they never do." As much as I tried, I couldn't stop the tears that started to slide down my cheeks. "Once a mother hurts her child, she keeps doing it. Because it's easy and it makes her feel strong." I didn't mean to keep talking, but I couldn't shut up. "She doesn't care about him. She didn't before and she won't now. Don't make me go back. Please. Please don't. You can't make him go back."

Mr. H. crossed over to me and pulled me up into a rough hug. I still couldn't stop.

"Don't make him go back. Don't send him back to her. Please. She makes him hurt. Don't make me go back."

Mr. Hassler never said anything, he just held me. And when my tears finally stopped, he still didn't say anything. He just patted me on the back, said "I'll see you tomorrow," and went down the hall to his room.

Breakfast the next morning was quiet. I didn't know what to say to Mr. H. After I had crawled in bed, I had cried myself to sleep. I hadn't broken down and cried like that since the last time my dad dropped me off at my mom's house. I wasn't able to stop myself from crying either time.

James came in as we were washing up the dishes. "Morning, Boss, Sean," he said, nodding to each of us.

"Morning," we replied at the same time. Mr. H. sounded only a little more lively than I did.

"What's the schedule for today, Boss?" James asked, sitting down.

"Well, I think Sean ought to finish the vegetable garden today. You can take care of the feeding, and then I thought maybe we ought to move the cattle from the far pasture into the east pasture, because the weatherman seems to think we've got a storm front coming in for the weekend."

"Fine with me," said James.

"And then," Mr. H. continued, "I thought you and Sean could start sorting and piling pumpkins for the elementary schools."

"Good enough," James said, standing up. "But when are we going to try Knicker with Manda again?"

Mr. H. looked at me. "I've decided that we're not going to."

"Okay, then," said James after a moment's hesitation. "You're the one who knows what you're doing."

"Why are we sorting pumpkins?" I asked, to cover my confusion.

"We donate pumpkins to schools each year."

"Yeah," James said, "and that's why you're here."

"Huh?"

"This ranch qualifies to receive community service because we make so many donations to the community. Pumpkins for Halloween, trees for Christmas, and then we run a youth summer camp for underprivileged children. So that's why we get you."

"Oh," I said, and went back to washing dishes.

Fertilizing the garden wasn't as bad that morning. It was getting colder out, so the stuff didn't stink nearly as much. I was really glad I took the jacket Mr. Hassler gave me.

I didn't want to let Knicker out into the paddock after feeding him because I thought it was too cold, but James said it would be good for him. Every once in a while as I was spreading the fertilizer, I'd catch a glimpse of him romping between the barns. It seemed James was right.

Sorting pumpkins was tough, but it wasn't nearly as hard as stacking the grain and hay had been yesterday.

"So what did you think of Boss's story yesterday?" James asked.

I shrugged. "It was pretty cool, I guess."

"It's too bad he didn't tell you all of it. If he had, you might think it's more than 'pretty cool.'"

"Oh? Then why don't you tell me the rest of the story?"

"Why? It wouldn't matter to you that he went against direct orders to go save his buddies."

"What do you mean, against direct orders?"

"He knew the men were in trouble, and so did his captain, but his captain had forbidden him to go back for them."

"Go back for them? I thought they were all together."

James shook his head. "No. The rest of the squad had already moved on, leaving those two to die or be taken prisoner."

"Why did the captain order Mr. H. not to go back? It doesn't make any sense."

"The captain didn't want any more of his men going back behind enemy lines."

"They were behind enemy lines?"

He nodded. "But Boss figured he didn't have anything to lose by going back for his buddies."

"Nothing to lose? What about his life?"

"Well, he was already wounded, so—"

"What?" This time my voice squeaked.

"Have you looked in the case with all of his badges and medals?"

"Yeah."

"Did you see the piece of shrapnel?"

"Yeah."

"They took that out of his arm after he carried the other wounded man back to the hospital."

I sat down in a daze. "I don't consider it above and beyond the call of duty," I could hear Mr. H. saying, "I consider it merely being human." My God! Not only had he saved two men, he had been injured at the time. In order to perform the rescue, he had been forced to go back behind enemy lines to find the wounded men!

James was grinning at me. "Kind of puts a different light on it, huh?"

"Kind of," I agreed weakly.

"C'mon," he said, slapping me on the back, "let's get these pumpkins sorted."

"Hey," I said suddenly. "That reminds me."

"What?"

"What about the bullet that's in the case?"

"What about it?"

"Why is it in there? There's got to be a story that goes with it too."

"Why don't you ask the boss?" James replied with a grin.

"I was going to, but I kind of have the feeling that you have a different story than the one I'll get from him."

"You catch on pretty quickly, Sean. But you need to ask him first. If he leaves details out again, I'll fill you in later."

"Good deal."

The more time I spent with James, the more okay he seemed. At first, I thought he was a jerk, just patronizing a kid. The more I got to know him, though, the more I realized I was the one who had been coming across as a jerk.

"Hey, James?"

"Yeah?"

"How many community service kids do you get here?"

He shrugged. "It changes from year to year. Sometimes we don't have anybody for weeks on end, sometimes we have to turn away kids who would be good working here."

"What do you mean, turn them away? I thought the judge just assigned people here."

He stopped sorting pumpkins, and looked at me like he was trying to decide whether or not to say something.

61

"Isn't that right? Can't the judge just assign people here?" I repeated.

"Yes and no," James answered. "Boss gets to have some say in the kids we get. He'll only take them if he thinks maybe he can help them. The judge usually knows what kind of kids would work well here, but Boss doesn't want more than one here at a time. He wants to be able to give you his full attention."

"Lucky me," I mumbled.

"Yeah, you are lucky," James said very seriously. "Give it a chance, Sean. Give Boss a chance. He wants to help you."

"What if I don't think I need any help?"

James shrugged and went back to sorting pumpkins. Yeah, I was definitely the one coming across as a jerk.

I took my time with Knicker that evening. I was trying to sort out how I felt about Mr. H. At first he had just seemed like an old fart who used the free labor of community service kids that his old fart judge friend passed over to him. Then, after I had spent a couple of days here, I thought that maybe he was trying to help me because he wanted to. Now I wasn't so sure. Now it seemed like something he just did as part of his job, not necessarily because he cared. He always tried to help the community service kids. Our relationship didn't seem so special anymore. I mean, I had thought that maybe he and I could get along, that maybe he would be willing to help me out. Now it didn't seem like any big deal. It was just what he did. I was just another community service kid to him.

Knicker butted me.

"Yeah, I know," I said, tugging playfully on his ears. "You and I are real buddies. You weren't planned. I got you." I hugged him. No one else did. And no one was going to take him away from me.

chapter nine

I tried to cook all of dinner that night, and as a result we ended up ordering a pizza. The smoke from my failed attempt at cooking was so bad we had to shut the doors between the kitchen and the rest of the house and open all of the kitchen windows. The temperature was supposed to go down to freezing that night, so it got pretty cold in there.

We had a good time at dinner though. We talked about Knicker's brother, who had just won his second race and seemed to be right on course for the state steeplechase in May.

We talked about skiing, something I had never had the chance to do.

We talked about school, something all three of us had had problems with. Mr. H. admitted that he had left school for good as a junior in high school. James had dropped out as a sophomore, but had gone back to get his GED and was currently enrolled at the local junior college.

James and I talked about the movies we had seen recently. Mr. H. said he hadn't been to a movie since the 1970s. I begged and pleaded with him to go to a movie with me the next day, but he just laughed and brushed it off.

"Why won't you go?"

He looked off into the distance. "I used to go, when I was younger. But after a while, things like that just don't matter. It's the things that you do in life that matter, not the things you see."

"Yeah, but there are some things that you may never get to really experience in life, but you can see them and learn about them in the movies," I argued.

"What have you learned in a movie that has actually helped you?" Mr. H. countered.

I thought hard, and the longer I thought, the harder it got. The longer I thought, the harder they laughed. But I knew I couldn't say I had learned how to hot-wire a car or how to tell the difference between an M16 and a sawed-off shotgun; that wouldn't have impressed Mr. H. In fact, he would have used that as another reason not to go.

"A bridle."

"What?" Mr. Hassler gasped out between laughs.

"I learned about bridles watching *Black Beauty*. And about bucking, and what happens to a horse if you give them too much cold water without cooling them off first."

Their laughter had slowed down while I was talking, but now James started all over again. "Oh, Boss, I think he's got you there."

"It ain't the same," he said calmly. "You may think you've learned about bridles, but I bet if I were to give you the gentlest mare and a bridle, you couldn't get it on her. And I virtually guarantee that if I was to put you on a hoss that bucks, you'd learn how to fly a lot faster than you'd learn how to ride."

"Yeah, but—"

"Sean, I'm old. The things I enjoy are a simple sunset with the smell of freshly cut hay in the air." He smiled at me. "I don't need to learn how to blow up a car."

I laughed, even though it spooked me how accurately he had read my thoughts.

There was a pause in our conversation, and I could tell we were getting ready to start dishes and then I'd be sent off to do homework.

"Hey, Mr. H.?"

"Hey, Sean?"

I looked at James, and he winked. It was okay then. He would stick to his bargain.

"Where'd the bullet in the case come from?"

Mr. H. shot a look at James.

"Don't look at me," James said, holding his hands up. "He asked me about it this afternoon. I told him to ask you."

I could tell Mr. H. didn't quite believe that James hadn't put me up to it. He just sat there chewing on his pipe. I wondered for a second how many pipe stems he went through in a month.

"Well, that bullet actually means more to me than anything else in the case." He looked at me. "But I'm not entirely sure you'll understand why."

"Give me a chance," I said.

He sighed. "It was, uh, November of '43. Real close to Thanksgiving.

Somehow the holidays always made things seem worse. I was miserable, so I wandered off from camp, just wanting to be alone, to have some thinking time. Unfortunately, I wasn't watching where I was walking, and I stumbled onto a German soldier, lying in a trench between some trees."

"What was he doing?"

"Hang on, I'll get there."

"Sorry," I mumbled.

Mr. H. took a couple of minutes to get his thoughts back in order.

"I didn't know if I was on his ground, or if he was on mine. And I guess it really didn't matter. We both pulled our guns on each other at the same time.

"Now, I had been in the service since '39, and I had seen plenty of action. But I had never been close enough to see the eyes of the men I was going to shoot before. I couldn't pull that trigger. I can only assume that the same was true for him. We both lowered our guns at exactly the same time."

"Wow, that was lucky," I said.

"Shhh!" James hissed, kicking me under the table. I realized that although James had heard these stories before, it wasn't something that Mr. H. talked about very often. James was as into the story as I was.

"As we lowered our guns," Mr. H. continued, unaware of my interruption or James's response, "he winced, and I realized that he was injured. I had been stationed in England and had been to France and Germany several times during the last four years, but the only language I knew how to speak was English."

"I dropped to my knees, so he would know I wasn't trying to hurt him, and crawled over to him. He must have been running and tripped. He had somehow landed on his own knife, and it had gone clean through his upper calf. I think he had also hit his head. I don't know how long he had been there, but he felt feverish.

"I helped him apply a tourniquet. He split his chocolate bar and clean drinking water with me. That may not seem like a big deal to you right now, but chocolate was very rare to have during the war. I hadn't had any in months. I helped him get closer to his camp, as close as I dared. And then I went and found him a large branch to use as a cane.

"When I took it to him, he took the last bullet out of his gun and gave it to me." He smiled. "It was Christmas and Thanksgiving all rolled into one.

It was the best meal and best gift I've ever had."

We sat quietly for a few minutes. I had questions I wanted to ask, but I was afraid to. I didn't want him taking them the wrong way. I was dying to know, though, how he could help a man who belonged to the enemy side. And, more importantly, how he had felt fighting the rest of the war. But I got the feeling that I needed to think about his story some on my own before I asked questions.

I could tell by the way James looked that Mr. Hassler had given me the whole story this time.

"And now," he said, getting up, "James and I will hit the dishes and you will hit the books. I want a rough draft from you by the time you go to bed tonight."

"Aw, come on. I can do it later. Besides, you're both doing fine with just a little more education than I've got now."

"The world's changing, Sean. I don't know if it's better or worse, but I do know that you need a college degree to do much of anything."

James nodded vigorously. "And it's easier to do if you've paid attention and done well in high school."

"I'm not going to get into any college anyway."

"Not with that attitude. And maybe college isn't what you want to do. But you're not going to come back saying that college wasn't a choice for you because you failed ninth-grade English."

I opened my mouth to complain, but he cut me off by just shaking his head slowly. "Boy, you would have made a great dad," I moaned.

He laughed.

"I can't believe you think it's funny to make a guy do homework on a Friday night," I said.

Mr. H. stopped laughing and turned around. "Bad habits are hard to break, and good ones are hard to get into. The sooner we get you into the habit of doing your homework, the better off you'll be. Now go on, get up there."

I actually did try to work on my rough draft that night. I tried at least four different beginnings before I admitted to myself that I just couldn't sit down to write. I did a few journal entries because they were easy and fast. I had a lot to say about what had happened to me in the last few days. Then I did a couple of sketches of Knicker for my art class. I knew I could get extra credit for them, and that might make up for the late papers and keep my grade at a B for the quarter.

Mr. H. scared the crud out of me when he set the plate of cookies and glass of milk on my desk. I just looked at him for a minute, then I burst out laughing. I really couldn't help it. "What's so funny?" he asked with a puzzled look on his face.

"Milk and cookies? Oh, man, where were you when I was in first grade?"

"Doesn't matter where I was. What matters is where I am."

I quit laughing. "Thanks. For everything. The cookies are just what I need to get through the next hour of homework."

He picked my sketches up. "What's this?"

I grinned. "Calculus."

He rolled his eyes at me, and I could tell he really wasn't in the mood for my humor.

"I'm in Art II. I don't have any textbooks here, so I can't do my other makeup work yet, but I can always get extra credit for my sketches. They help me keep my grade up."

He held my second sketch under the lamp and looked at it critically before he handed it back. "Nice job with his face, but his fetlocks should be just a tad shorter," he said, pointing. "Makes him look out of proportion."

"You mean his legs?"

"The lower part, about where our ankles are."

Just as I was going to ask him another question, the phone rang.

"Back to work," he said to me as he moved toward the door. "Remember, I want to see that rough draft tonight."

I sighed and put my drawings to the side. I got out some more notebook paper and then looked at my notes. I had started going through my lists, numbering them so I could go back and group similar ideas together when I felt someone's eyes on my back.

I didn't turn around. "What, did you forget to leave me my blankie too?"

No answer. Then I did turn around. Mr. H. had a funny expression on his face.

"What?" He didn't say anything. "What happened? Who was on the phone?"

"Get your jacket and meet me out front," he said heavily, starting down the hall.

"Knicker? Did something happen to Knicker?" I yelled after him.

"No," he called back. "Just come on."

I shoved my feet into my shoes without untying them and hurried down the hall, mystified. *Of course*, I thought, *he wouldn't have gotten a phone call about Knicker*. So who had called? What would have made the expression on his face look so cold and hard?

By the time I got outside, he had pulled the truck up. I got in, and he started driving before I even pulled the door all the way shut. I sat and waited for him to tell me what was going on. Finally it dawned on me that I would have to wait a long time before he would volunteer any information.

"Where are we going?" I asked. He didn't seem to want to tell me who was involved, so I thought I'd be sly and try to figure it out myself.

"Hospital."

That stopped me. "Who are we going to see?"

He took a deep breath. And then he took another one.

"Who's there? James? Did something happen to James on his way home?"

He shook his head again. "No, no, nothing like that." He paused. "I guess there's no easy way to say this. We're going to see your mom."

"Oh," I said, and turned to look out the window. I could feel his eyes on me again, waiting for an outburst. But I really didn't feel much of anything. "You can slow down," I said. "It's not worth a ticket and there are always speed traps here."

"Did you hear me, Sean? I said your mother's in the hospital."

"Yeah, I heard you. Did they tell you why she's there?"

He shook his head.

"Well, my guess is they found her passed out in some bar and couldn't get her to wake up. They'll probably have to pump her stomach, and she'll be home tomorrow." *And,* I thought to myself, *I'm glad I won't have to be there this time. She is always meanest when they try to dry her out.*

Mr. H. had slowed down by the time we passed the cop who was hiding under the bridge.

"Speed trap. Told you!"

"Thank you for the warning," he said as he watched his rearview mirror.

"No problem."

We were quiet for a few more minutes. I could tell he wanted to ask something, but by then I wasn't in the mood to keep the conversation going.

"How long have your parents been divorced?" he asked finally.

"'Bout nine years," I said, shrugging.

"Your mom has full custody?"

I nodded. "Dad's got visiting privileges. Not that he uses them."

"Where does he live?"

"He just moved to Ft. Lewis two months ago."

"But you said last Friday was the first time in two years that you had seen him."

"Yep."

That shut him up for a while. I mean, what do you say to a kid whose father lives only an hour away and still is too busy to come visit? For that matter, what do you think when you're that kid? I found that the easiest thing was not to think of it at all. I think Mr. Hassler came to the same conclusion, because he changed the subject. Well, sort of.

"Your mom drinks a lot?"

"You could say that."

"How many times has she been in the hospital to get her stomach pumped?"

"Well," I said, thinking, "about four or five."

"This has been since your parents' divorce?"

"Oh, no, this has just been since I was in junior high. I don't remember how many times it happened before that."

I had heard of people clenching their teeth, but this was the first time I had seen it personally.

"Does your dad know about this?"

I shrugged again. "I guess maybe the social workers told him. I don't know."

"You've seen social workers?"

"Oh, lots of times. Especially when mom's in rehab."

"Well then, damn it, why are you still living with her?"

I was quiet for a few minutes. I didn't have an answer for him, and we were pulling into the hospital parking lot. I didn't want to go in there.

"Do we have to?"

"Yeah, Sean, I think we do."

"Great." I took a deep breath. "I'm the only thing she has, since my dad walked out on us. He left us both without options. I have to tell the social workers that she cares about me, because there's nowhere else for me to go. And, of course," I laughed a little because it stopped the tears, "I guess she at least gives a rat's tail about me. I mean, she at least cares enough to lie and *say* she cares about me." I slid out of the truck and slammed the door.

The bright white of the hospital hallway was broken by an occasional large print hanging on the wall, probably someone's misguided attempt to make the hospital seem less impersonal and threatening. It failed miserably. No one would possibly consider hanging those things in a home.

I went up to the ER desk.

"May I help you, honey?" a middle-aged nurse asked me as she cracked her gum.

"Yeah, my mom was checked in tonight. I'm just here to say hi."

"Her name?"

"Candy Kane. With a K."

The nurse raised her eyebrows, but she was one of the few who didn't actually make a smart-aleck remark. I was grateful.

"Um, let's see....She checked in at seven-thirty. She's in...oh, dear, are you here alone?"

"Does it matter?"

"Well, honey," she started. It really bugs me when complete strangers call me honey. "She's in critical condition. No visitors allowed. Do you have someone to stay with tonight?"

"What happened to her?" I asked at the same time a hand came down on my shoulder. "Yes, he does," Mr. H. said to the nurse.

She immediately focused her attention on him. "Are you his guardian?"

"I am."

I looked at him and he dropped me a wink.

"I'll get a doctor. He'll be able to tell you more about her condition."

We headed to the waiting room.

"Sean?"

I turned around and there was Mrs. Walker, looking frazzled.

"What are you doing here?" we both said at the same time.

She laughed, sort of. "My husband managed to slice his hand cutting a bagel. He's in getting stitches right now. What are you doing here? Are you all right?"

"Oh, yeah, I'm fine. I'm just here to see my mom. She's sick. Might be pneumonia." I'd been lying for her for so long, the words just popped out of my mouth without any thought.

Mr. H. gave me a funny look. He opened his mouth, but for some reason, he didn't say anything.

"I'm sorry to hear that."

I shrugged.

There was this really awkward silence. Then Mrs. Walker said as brightly as she could, "Well, I better get back to him. See you on Monday, Sean."

"Bye," Mr. H. and I said.

While we were waiting for the doctor, Mr. H. bought a candy bar and soda for me and a coffee for himself. The waiting room didn't do much for my appetite; it was a nasty green with orange trim. The hospital decorator should have paid that extra dollar to get a professional opinion.

"Thanks for the chocolate," I said, holding up the candy bar.

"You're welcome. It's not quite milk and cookies, but it will have to do."

I grinned. "Well, our country may not be on chocolate rations right now, but I don't have chocolate very often. I think I even like it a little better than the milk and cookies."

He smiled back at me. "I would give you the chocolate even if we were on rations."

Neither of us said anything for a few minutes, and the only sound was that of the clock ticking, steadily counting down the time.

"Hey," I said suddenly. "You won't get in trouble, will you?"

"For giving you chocolate?" he asked, his brows drawn together in confusion.

"No," I said with a laugh. "For lying about being my guardian."

He shifted in his chair. "Well, I didn't really lie, you know. It was more like stretching the truth."

"I don't get it."

"It's simple, really. I told you that I had arranged for you to stay at the ranch this week instead of going to in-house, and in order to do that, I had to agree to take temporary custody of you."

"What's that mean?"

"It means that legally I'm responsible for you and your actions. It means that in the court's eyes, I'm your parent while you're on my ranch."

I looked at him. I didn't know what to say. He wasn't required to take care of me; he had volunteered to do it. He could have kicked me out whenever he wanted to. But, even though he hadn't known what I was doing, even though I hadn't told him what was going on, he accepted me. He hadn't been ordered by the court to pay child support, but he bought me candy bars. He hadn't yelled at me for burning our dinner; he came up to offer encouragement while I was doing homework instead.

"Sean Parker?" A man in a white jacket was waiting at the door.

"Yeah," I said, and Mr. H. and I stood up.

He led us down a quieter section of the hallway, stopping in front of an interior window. I could see a woman lying on a bed on the other side. She had tubes coming out everywhere. Little electronic devices beeped and flashed all around her. It took me a couple of minutes to recognize her as my mother.

"What's her condition?" Mr. Hassler asked briskly.

"Critical right now, but stabilizing. We should be able to downgrade her no later than tomorrow morning."

"What happened to her?" Mr. H. looked at me kinda funny and then put an arm around me and squeezed. I guess I must have looked like I felt—like I did the time he pulled the chair out from under me.

"Kidney failure. And I think her liver's got some problems. She's been doing quite a bit of habitual drinking, by the looks of it."

The possibility of life without my mother had always been in the corner of my mind, as a kind of fantasy, where I could be happy. But I had talked with a friend who had come back after a stint as a runaway, and I knew that my home, as bad as it was, was still a home, a place I could go, a place where I could usually find food. If my mother died, where would I go? It was the same question that had kept me lying to the social workers whenever they were called.

Mr. H. led me over to a chair and had me sit down.

"Do you have any information on the type of health insurance she has?"

Mr. H. and I both shook our heads.

"She doesn't have any."

Startled, I looked up and saw my father looking through the window at her. There was no expression on his face. "Send the bill to me."

"And who would you be?" asked the doctor.

"I'm her ex-husband."

"Oh. I see. Well, sir, that will certainly help, but she will need follow-up treatment and a transplant pretty soon. Perhaps you could help me fill out some paperwork and see if we can get her some kind of financial assistance."

"Fine."

I had finally found my voice. "What are you doing here?"

My father sighed. "Sean, this will probably take a while. Take a cab home and I'll come pick you up in the morning." He fished out his wallet and tossed a twenty on my lap.

I stood up without touching it, letting it fall to the floor.

"Why are you here? Who called you?"

He gave me a quick look that said he didn't want to waste his time talking to me. "The hospital called me. I'm still on her financial support list." He ran a hand through his thinning hair. "Pick up the money and go on home." He was staring through the glass at my mother.

"Dad, this is Dave Hassler."

My father looked at Mr. H. blankly and gave a little nod, ignoring Mr. H.'s outstretched hand.

"Dad," I said. "Dad," I repeated, louder this time. I waited until he was looking at me.

"I've been staying with Mr. H. for the week. I'm going back for the rest of the weekend."

"Don't be stupid. It was nice of Mr. uh…," he fumbled, unable to remember Mr. Hassler's name. "It was nice of him to let you stay, but now you need to go home and pack. You don't need to bother him anymore. I'll pick you up tomorrow and you can stay with me until we figure out what kind of permanent arrangement we can work out together."

"No," I said, taking a step toward him. He actually looked up and saw me for the first time. "I'm going with Mr. H. I've got work to do. When I'm done, I'll call you."

"Sean, this is not open for discussion."

"Right, Dad, it's not. You've been out of my life for years. You don't just come back into my life and start giving me orders."

"Young man, I'm your father," he began.

"Oh, really? And when did you get this news flash? Because you sure haven't been my father for the last nine years."

"I'm sorry the divorce upset you, but this is hardly the place—"

"It wasn't the divorce!" I yelled. "It was you. You kept taking me back to her. I told you how bad it was, but you were too busy to fit me back into your schedule." I could feel the hot tears on my face, but I couldn't stop, not yet. "Well, now, *Dad,* I've got my life going. And I'm not going to let you butt in and screw it up all over again." I shoved past him.

He reached out to stop me, and Mr. Hassler stepped toward him, blocking his reach.

I could hear their voices growing more distant as I went down the hall. Finally, when I stepped outside into the calming darkness, I escaped their voices completely.

eaning against the side of the truck, I could feel the wind cool my burning cheeks off quickly, and dry them as well. I tried to steady my breathing. My heart was pounding in my ears. I didn't care what my father thought. I didn't want to go live with him. All I wanted to do was live happily-ever-after at Carbondale Ranch. But since I knew that wouldn't happen, I was pulling for just being able to stay for the next week or so. And I was already trying to figure out a way to be there for the summer camp, either as a camper or as a worker.

I had accidentally left the jacket inside. I tried the truck doors, hoping to get in out of the wind, but they were locked. I walked around the truck nervously, and it helped keep me warm. Once, twice, five times. I walked back to the hospital and then turned around five feet from the door. Walked back to the truck. Went all the way to the emergency room door then back to the truck again. What could be taking so long? I walked around the truck two more times. *Okay, fine, this time I'm going in,* I promised myself. *I must look like a moron walking back and forth out here.*

I got halfway back to the hospital door when it swung open and Mr. Hassler walked out. When he got within a couple of feet, he tossed me the jacket.

"Ready to go?" he asked, striding right past me.

"Uh, sure," I said, pulling on the jacket and hurrying to keep up with him.

I looked back over my shoulder three times as we were pulling out of the parking lot. He wasn't saying anything, and the whole situation felt wrong. Like we were running away from something.

My teeth started chattering, in spite of the jacket. He glanced at me and turned the heater on, but he still didn't say anything.

I was dying of curiosity but I didn't want to give him the satisfaction of knowing it was bothering me. Any normal person would just tell you what had happened after you left. Mr. H. was just being a jerk, and I wasn't going to ask him about it.

"Hey," I said with half a smile. "It looks like I got out of writing my paper again."

Mr. H. grunted.

"It's no big deal anyway. It's not like I'm failing or anything; I'm getting by."

"Life is not about getting by, Sean. It's about meeting challenges and giving everything and everyone all that you have."

"Maybe it used to be," I retorted. "But it's not like that anymore. People who work all the time get all stressed out and never have the time to enjoy life. I'm not ever going to be like that."

He frowned. "No, you certainly aren't."

I sat back and relaxed. At least he wasn't going to fight me on that.

He continued, "You'll just get by, and you'll have to work all the time at a low-paying job and never have the opportunity to decide if you want to take the time off to enjoy life. It will be financially impossible for you to take time off."

I glared at him. "I'll make a good living."

"Doing what?"

"How should I know. I'm only fifteen, for Pete's sake!"

"Only fifteen," he mimicked. "Too young to know what you want to do, but old enough to have decided you don't care about anything or anyone. Old enough to have decided you're not going to do anything with your life because all you need to do is 'get by.'"

"Pull over."

"What?"

My lips felt like ice and I was shaking all over, but I repeated myself. "Pull over. I'll just walk back to my mother's house from here. I'm not going to listen to this stuff from my father, and I'm sure not going to listen to it from some old fart who's a complete stranger."

"Boy, you've really got that all wrong," he said, shaking his head.

"Pull over!"

"Like hell," he growled.

I reached for the door handle. I didn't care how fast we were going, I was getting out. As soon as I moved, though, he slammed his hand down on my thigh just above my knee and squeezed. Hard. The pain was unreal.

"Don't even think about it," he snarled.

"This is kidnapping!" I yelled. "I'll sue! This is assault! Your butt is mine!"

He did pull over then, although it was more of a sudden swerve. And suddenly I knew I had crossed some line I had never wanted to cross. I threw myself out of the truck before it came to a complete stop, and bolted through the field.

He caught me. I don't know how, but he did. Well, actually, he tripped me, and kind of landed on top of me. But he yanked me up again by the collar before I really felt the impact. He shook me a few times, his face just inches from mine.

"I told you before, when you talk to people who care about you, you treat them with respect. You put effort forward and give them what they've given to you. Do you understand me?" He was really yelling at me.

"Yessir," I ground out sarcastically. "You're giving me so much respect right now, I don't know how I missed it."

"Where do you come off, pulling this attitude with me? Huh? Who do you think you are?" He shook me again under the freezing stars. "Do you think you're the only one who hurts and that makes you better than everyone else?"

"I know I'm not the only one who hurts," I yelled back, "but I'm tired of being hurt and I'm not going to take it from anyone anymore! Let go of me! You don't care! You can get the next kid they bust to come in to shovel crap for you! I don't matter to you; getting your work done for free is all that's important to you."

He released me suddenly, and I dropped to the ground. Towering above me with his hands on his hips, he yelled at me so loud his voice was shaking.

"I just put not only myself on the line, I put my whole ranch, my whole life, on the line for you! You don't want to go to daddy, you cry, so I step in and fight to get you the right to stay with me. And then, all you can think about is skating by in life. You don't want to do a damn thing if it involves work and effort. Is that why you didn't want to go with your father? Huh? Because, by God, I will not coddle a boy who's simply being selfish!"

"I am not being selfish!" I screamed at him. "You're just upset because now you're the one who stands to lose something. I've been losing my whole life!"

"You made it sound like your life at home was bad. Now I wonder if you were just too much of a pansy to handle life and you're the one who made your home life bad."

I stared up at him. "Oh, yeah, like you know anything about my home life."

"I'd know more about your home life if you cared enough to talk about it." He had stopped yelling. Sort of.

"You say you've been losing your whole life," he said. "Well, I've got news for you, bucko, you've been losing because you don't have the guts to try to win. It's easier for you to roll over and say you've lost, so you don't even try to win. And then you look for pity.

"Well, you're not going to get any pity from me. I've given you all the chances I know how to give. You can't even say thank you, probably because it takes too much effort."

In the background, I could hear the truck engine running. The air was frosty, the ground was hard, and the clouds made the night seem like a black hell.

"Forget it!" He threw his hands up in disgust. "Go throw your life away. Go sulk at dad's and shut yourself off from everyone." He turned and kicked at a weed at his feet. "You've made it clear you don't want me. Why should I want you?"

He turned and walked toward the road. He didn't understand. No one understood. I felt completely alone again. I didn't like it.

I got up and dusted myself off. I broke into a light jog to catch up with him.

I reached the passenger side of the truck just as he was opening the driver's door. He stopped and looked at me over the roof. I held his gaze as long as I could, which wasn't very long.

I opened my mouth to apologize, but I just couldn't. Instead, I said, "I'd like to be able to stay at the ranch until I'm done with my community service. I'll do any chores you give me, and I won't complain." Mr. H. didn't say anything. "And I'll do my homework. I'll do the best I know how to do."

He looked at me for a long time. I tried to stay still, but I had a hard time keeping my teeth from chattering.

"You planning on doing any more cooking?" he asked.

"Only if you tell me to."

"I don't think I can afford pizzas every night for the next couple of weeks," Mr. H. said dryly.

"I'll try to be more careful and pay attention in the kitchen."

"If you come with me now, there will be no more back talk, and you will give 100 percent to each job I give you, whether I tell you to give 100 percent or not."

I nodded, bouncing on my feet, trying to stay warm.

"Well, then, let's go. Six-thirty comes early in the morning."

I just enjoyed the warmth of the truck for the rest of the drive to the ranch. My eyes kept closing, and then my head would drop forward until I snapped it back.

The cold air on the walk to the house woke me up a little, but I was still exhausted. We climbed the stairs silently, and then he turned toward his end of the hall.

"Mr. H.?"

He stopped but didn't turn around.

"What did you mean when you said that you had put yourself and the ranch on the line for me?

His shoulders dropped just a little. "Your father thinks he can get a lawsuit out of this."

I didn't understand. "Why?" I asked. "What did you say?"

"I told him that I had been given partial custody for the rest of the week and that you were still doing community service for me."

"But if that's all true, where would a lawsuit come from?"

He bowed his head. "When we were talking, neither of us used the most polite tones or words we could find. I believe the charges he has in mind are slander and assault."

"Assault?"

He still hadn't turned around. "He said something, and I hit him."

"What did he say?"

"It doesn't matter."

"It was about me, wasn't it?"

"It doesn't matter, Sean. I lost my temper. I shouldn't have."

"Mr. H." He still didn't turn around. "Dave," I said, and this time he turned slowly. I waited until he looked up at me.

"Thank you. For everything. You've...." I stopped, took a deep breath, and started over. "Thank you for giving me your chocolate."

This time I was the one who turned away with my head down.

"Good night, Sean. We'll see you in the morning."

chapter eleven

I fell asleep very quickly, but I woke up at four in the morning and couldn't go back to sleep. I tossed and turned for almost forty-five minutes before I decided to stop fighting it and get up and get dressed.

I sat at the desk and worked on my paper for about an hour. I quit when I glanced out the window and saw the sky turning purple and pink. I crept down the stairs without making a sound and grabbed the jacket on my way out.

Even though it hadn't taken me long to get down the stairs and outside, the sky was already turning gold. The long grass that hugged the path to the stable was bending under the weight of the dew. Before long, it would be frost instead.

Knicker was up when I got to his stall. He seemed excited to see me even though his eyes weren't completely open. Then he yawned. It was the funniest thing I had ever seen. I don't know why, but I guess I never thought horses would yawn.

I put the halter on him, and he followed me out into the paddock. I'd like to think he followed me because he liked me, but I think it probably had more to do with the fact that he wanted the bottle I was carrying.

Head down, tail up; head up, tail down. He yanked and pulled on the bottle, first shoving his head into me, then backing off a few steps. When the bottle was empty, he stood next to me, leaning against my side, blinking his eyes. He looked more than just satisfied. He looked happy, content. We were both learning how to enjoy that feeling at the ranch.

We watched the sunrise together. Well, I watched it. He sort of dozed for a few minutes, and then he ran around the paddock a bit. He'd kick up his back heels and then run as fast as he could, stopping abruptly to sniff a clump of thistles. Then he'd be off again, racing his shadow, and jumping out of his skin when a rabbit popped up in front of him.

I enjoyed having the time alone, time I could use to think. I felt like I had been transplanted into a fairy-tale world. I mean, here I was, at a great ranch, working with a guy who cared about me. Not because he had to, not because he would get anything from it, but for some other reason. For the life of me, I couldn't figure out why Mr. H. wanted to help me. I was just glad that he did.

I felt embarrassed about last night, but I didn't know what I could do about it. And although I had acted pretty awful, at least I had found out that even though Mr. H. got lots of kids during the year, he didn't consider us just a bunch of faces. He really cared.

I wanted to believe the fairy tale would last forever, but I knew better. Happy endings are only found in Hollywood. But that didn't mean my ending had to be bad. I probably wouldn't be able to stay with Mr. Hassler like I wanted to, but I could do something other than just go back home. I could go do something. I just didn't quite know what. Maybe my dad and I could work something out.

We stayed out there for twenty minutes before I figured it was probably time to head back up to the house. When I called Knicker to me and started to lead him back to his stall, I realized there was nothing wrong with leaving him where he could stretch his legs and get exercise for the morning. I left him nickering at me over the paddock fence.

I didn't see James's truck when I got to the house, so I slipped inside as quietly as I could. I didn't know what time it was, or what time Mr. H. got up, and I didn't want to be the one to wake him up.

Then I heard his voice. I almost said good morning before I realized he was on the phone. He was talking quietly, probably trying not to wake me up.

"Yeah, Frank, I'm sorry to wake you so early on a Saturday morning, but I need to talk to you about the kid.... Yes, Sean Parker.... No, no, he's doing fine work, and I really appreciate you helping me get him around the school's in-house policy....This is a new problem.... Well, his mother was admitted to the hospital last night.... No, well, look, I've got to make this quick, so how about you get the rest of the story by coming over this afternoon?... Yeah, it's pretty important.... Well, I think his father's planning a lawsuit.... I kind of hit him last night.... No, not Sean, I hit his father.... Yeah, yeah, me and my temper.... But Frank, he was standing there, calmly telling me that I shouldn't spend extra time on a worthless case like his son.... I couldn't believe it either.... And I've got this feeling Sean's mother isn't exactly—" Mr. Hassler broke off abruptly as he turned around and saw me standing in front of him.

"Um, Frank, can you come over this afternoon?... I'd appreciate it.... Yeah, I've got to go now.... Twelve o'clock.... Bye." He hung up the phone slowly, never taking his eyes off me.

I dropped the jacket over the back of the couch. "What should I start for breakfast?" I asked, heading to the kitchen.

"Sean," he reached out and stopped me by putting a hand on my shoulder. "How much did you hear?"

"Probably all of it."

"I'm sorry. I really didn't want you to hear any of it."

I shrugged. "No big deal," I said, continuing on to the kitchen. "What? Don't look so surprised. You don't really think that's the first time I've heard that, do you?"

He followed me into the kitchen and sat down at the table. He looked like he was at a complete loss.

"Of course," I said, rummaging through the fridge for the milk and orange juice, "I haven't heard it from him. I haven't heard anything from him for years. Now I guess I know why."

I poured two glasses of orange juice and set them on the table. Mr. Hassler still didn't say anything. I dug the pancake mix out of the cupboard, and went back to the fridge for the eggs.

"Sean."

I looked at him.

"Come here. Sit down. Please."

"Let me get breakfast—"

"Breakfast can wait," he cut in. "Please sit down."

I sat down.

He closed his eyes briefly. "I didn't want you to hear what your father said because I was afraid you might believe it. Now you say you've heard it a lot. Do you believe what you hear?"

"Everyone else does."

"I'm asking if you do."

"It doesn't matter what I think when everyone else has already made up their minds."

"Yes it does!"

"No it doesn't! Even when I believe I can do something, it doesn't matter. Okay, I believe I'm smart and can do well in school. So I study for my test. And then I'm accused of cheating because I got an A. I like the research assignment, so I spend four hours writing the paper, and then I get asked who wrote it for me. I go out for sports, and I get cut because things have been stolen from the locker room, and I'm the only nonpreppy, nonjock on the team, so I must have been the one doing it. It doesn't matter what I believe, not when everyone else has already decided for me."

He put his head in his hands. "Oh, God, you really are me all over again," he muttered.

"What?"

"Sean, I grew up during the Depression. Things were bad for everyone, but they were really bad for my family. We had a history of being drunks, cheaters, thieves, and lazy bums who would never amount to a damn thing. My grandfather was that way. My father was that way. So were both of my older brothers. I decided I didn't want to be that way." He took a deep breath. "I lived in a town of 400 people. I spent my whole life trying to prove myself better than my family. In a town that small, it's not an easy task."

I thought about that. My junior high had 600 students, and there were six junior highs in our district. To live where the entire town had only 400 people.... "That's a small town," I said. "I bet everybody knew what kind of person you were going to be."

"They *thought* they knew," he corrected. "I was out to prove them wrong."

"It sounds impossible."

"It felt impossible," he agreed. "So many times I thought I couldn't do it. So many times I decided that maybe I should just quit and be what they wanted me to be. It would be easier." He shook his head. The small smile on his lips didn't reach his eyes. "But then one day a set of diamond cuff links were stolen. They belonged to the mayor. There were six of us in the town who had been working in his office, cleaning. We were rounded up. They started grilling me right away. I held my ground. They couldn't get any information out of any of us, so we were released. But small towns have their own way of doing unofficial trials, and I had already been tried and convicted. For the rest of the week, I could feel the town's hatred every time I walked down the street."

I knew exactly how that felt.

"So anyway, a week later, they caught a kid trying to pawn the cuff links in the next town. It turned out to be the mayor's own son."

"You're kidding!"

"I'm serious. The next day, I was confused when the mayor called me and asked me to drop by his house. I went on my way to work. He apologized and said that he had read me wrong, and that he had been doing it for a long time. Then he pulled twenty dollars out and tried to hand it to me."

"Tried to?" I leaned forward in my chair. "You didn't take it?"

"No. For two reasons. First, if I suddenly had money, people would question where it came from, like, what did I steal this time? Second, I didn't want him thinking I could be bought."

"What do you mean, 'bought'?"

"I didn't want him thinking that just by giving me money he could make everything better. I wasn't looking for money. I wanted to be…" He broke off, searching for the word.

"Respected? Understood? Accepted?"

"Yes," he said, nodding with a smile. "All of those."

"What did he say when you didn't take the money?"

"He asked me what I wanted to do with my life, since I was obviously struggling to stay on the straight and narrow path. He said that I was still on it, he knew that, but he also knew I was struggling. I told him all I was trying to do was hang on for another two years—until I was eighteen—and then I was going to enlist."

Mr. H. stopped for a drink of orange juice. "He asked me if I really wanted to enlist. I said of course, because that was the only way I was going to get out of that town and have a chance to get somewhere in my life. Then he asked if I would go now if I had the chance."

"But you were only sixteen! You didn't have that choice."

"That's what I thought. But he said he could pull some strings and get me in right away. When I went home that night, I told my family that I was going to leave the next week to go get a better job. My father laughed at me. It was an angry, scary laugh. He told me he was sick of me trying to act like I was better than the rest of them. We had a huge fight, and I slept in the back shed for the rest of the week."

He sighed and smiled. "I left town that Monday, and I've never looked back."

I started laughing. "So you were illegal in the army."

"Technically, yes. But the point is, Sean, that if you believe in yourself, it doesn't matter what others think."

"So, what, you want me to go enlist?"

"You've got an advantage. It's easier these days in a town this size to move to where people don't know you. Now it's easier to find a career with ways to advance that are outside of the military. You can do it, Sean. If you believe in yourself and if you decide that's what you want to do."

I sat quietly for a few minutes. I must not have looked convinced, because he leaned forward and said softly, "I lied. I did look back once. I only went back because my mother had passed away, and I wanted to pay my respects. Then I went to town to see my father. He was still living in the same run-down house. Only by that time, it was more like a shack. I stayed there for fifteen minutes."

Mr. Hassler's voice dropped a notch, and he looked down at his feet. "The whole time I was there, my father tried to belittle me, tried to make me feel worthless again. Understand, at this time I had been gone for fifteen years. I was married and holding a steady job at Burlington. I left a fifty-dollar bill on the kitchen table for my father as I walked out. And on my way out of town, I suddenly realized something."

He looked up at me. "People had been putting me down all my life because they could tell I could be something if I wanted to be. They didn't want me to succeed. That's why they made my life hell. If I could succeed where they didn't, then they were weaker than I was. So they tried to stop me.

"Sean, a lot of people can tell you can succeed. Some of them will try to stop you now from even trying. Don't let them. Come back in twenty years and be able to buy your father's company. Don't sink into what they think you are."

I dropped my eyes to look at the floor. I didn't want Mr. Hassler to know how good that idea felt. I could do it. I could prove Mr. H. right and my mother and father wrong all at the same time.

The kitchen door slammed and I jumped.

"Hey, where's breakfast? Here I am, running late and absolutely starving, and there's no breakfast?" James sat down at the table as I got up.

He looked at us. "What's going on?"

"Nothing," I said quickly.

"It was a late night," Mr. H. explained. "We got a phone call about nine, telling us Sean's mother is in the hospital."

"Oh, jeez, I'm sorry to hear that, Sean," he said as I handed him some orange juice.

"Thanks."

"She gonna be okay?"

I shrugged.

"We don't know," Mr. H. said. "She was in critical condition, but they think she'll recover. Her kidneys failed."

"Oh."

I started the pancakes.

"Well, I thought you and I could exercise ten of the riding ponies today, and then get the other ten tomorrow," Mr. H. said briskly. "And we'll have Sean start the cornfield this morning."

I nodded.

"Then this afternoon, Sean, I want you to work with Knicker some more with the halter and start grooming him. James will show you which soft brush to use."

This time I didn't even try to hold back a grin.

Things were going to be okay. I could find the right track here. Mr. H. would help me stay there.

chapter twelve

The cornfield was the field closest to the main road. I felt kind of funny driving the tractor around where I could be seen. Carbondale Ranch was off the beaten path for most of my friends, but I was still worried that someone I knew might come out this way. I really didn't want to be seen and then labeled "tractor boy" or something stupid like that at school.

But after a while I got into what I was doing, and I quit watching the road. I was having a great time. If anyone had told me a week ago that I would enjoy my community service, I would have laughed at them. Actually, I would have laughed at the idea of me liking any kind of job.

Spreading manure wasn't a glamorous job. It required just the right amount of effort and concentration to make it interesting, but not enough to make it frustrating. The first day I used the spreader, I didn't pay enough attention, and it jammed. By the time I noticed the jam, I had to go back and redo half the field.

The air was brisk and cold. I must have been getting used to the job, because it didn't smell that much. Well, I mean, it smelled, but it didn't stink. It kind of had a warm, earthy smell. The sky was calm with blankets of thick gray clouds, and the forecast was calling for snow by Sunday evening. It was only about forty-five degrees, but it felt really good. The border of the field had trees planted every five to ten feet, and their leaves had almost completely changed to gold and orange.

While I was using the spreader, I saw several rabbits leaving their homes just as I was about to drop a load on them. They were cute, but nothing spectacular. Then, just as I was getting ready to go in for lunch, I saw him. A fox.

He was sitting on the edge of the field, just watching me. He looked like a strange combination of cat and dog. He was sitting up straight, with his tail wrapped around his front paws. His coat was a dull orange, not the bright red I always thought foxes had.

We watched each other for a few minutes, and it started to get creepy. I even got goose bumps. It really felt like he was looking at me for a reason. Then he turned his head to the side for a moment. I looked the same way, to see what he had heard or smelled, and when I looked back, he was gone.

I looked back again to where the fox had looked, and this time I saw what had scared him away.

Rick was walking along the road by the field. I froze. I knew if I ran, it would definitely get his attention. Rick was, in a lot of ways, like a bird of prey. He only caught on to things if there was action around, and his brain was approximately the same size as a bird's. If he thought I was just some farm-boy jerk, he probably wouldn't pay any attention to me. He glanced at me, and then looked back to the road.

I slid off the tractor and headed toward the house.

"Yo, Sean!"

I jumped. He had bellowed really loud. I turned around slowly. He was standing on the second bar of the fence, leaning forward.

"I don't know where you've been, but you better not come back to school! I'll kill you, man!"

I flipped him the bird and just started walking to the house again. I made myself walk slowly, even though I wanted desperately to break into a run. Rick didn't make threats lightly. When I got to the end of the field, I turned and looked back. He was still there, just watching me. No, he didn't make threats lightly at all.

I wandered back to the main house, stopping to say hi to the little black and white calf that got me in trouble the first day I was here. Then I detoured to the stables to check on Knicker. He was trying to chew on the hay. I took that as a good sign. He needed to get off the bottle quickly, because it took valuable time to feed him by hand like that. I liked doing it, but I wasn't sure how long I'd be around.

There was a strange car in front of the house when I came back from the stable. I went directly to the bathroom to wash up, and then to the kitchen to help James.

"Where's Mr. H.?" I asked, pouring three glasses of milk.

James set another empty glass in front of me. "Pour four. The judge is here, and it looks like he'll be staying for lunch."

"Oh," I said, feeling a knot start in the bottom of my stomach. "How long has he been here?"

"About an hour. Oh, hey, the hospital called. Your mom's now in stable condition. She'll be released in a few days."

"Okay. Thanks."

We finished making the soup and sandwiches in relative silence. It was a comfortable silence though. We were both concentrating on working and waiting for Mr. H. to come in.

When he did, the judge who sentenced me to community service was right behind him. He walked up to me, stopping only six inches away. We locked gazes. After Mr. H., though, this guy was easy to stare down.

He gave one quick nod. "You're looking good, boy. I knew Dave would bring you around faster than anyone else. That's why I made sure you came here, instead of some other place."

"Sean's been working hard," Mr. H. said from the kitchen table.

"Which is a big change from hardly working," James said, elbowing me.

We sat down to eat, and I almost felt like it was the first day all over again. I didn't say much of anything, and I felt all out of place. I tensed each time the judge brought up the name of a former community service kid. Mr. H. could always explain exactly where the kid was and what he was doing.

Toward the end of the meal, Mr. H. turned to me. "How'd the corn-field look?"

"Good," I said, "I got most of it done. I should be able to finish with no problem tomorrow." Mr. Hassler hadn't taken his eyes off me. It was the first time in the conversation that he had given me his undivided attention. "I saw a fox."

He raised his eyebrows. "By the cornfield?"

I nodded.

"Hmmm, that's unusual. We haven't had any foxes here for a few years. Too much traffic and too many big dogs running around. Not that I've minded not having foxes, though."

"What's wrong with foxes? I thought he looked kinda cool."

Mr. H. shrugged and looked a little uncomfortable. James and the judge were grinning at him. "I don't know," he said, "Maybe it sounds silly, but foxes have always bothered me. They just seem…"

"Creepy?" I asked, remembering the goose bumps.

"Exactly," he agreed. "They seem creepy. And sometimes it seemed to me that they brought bad luck. So I always kept a couple of dogs around, in case the traffic wasn't enough to keep the foxes away."

"Abe was the last dog you had here, wasn't he?" the judge asked.

James and Mr. Hassler said yes at the same time.

"And how long has it been since Abe died?" asked the judge.

"Just over a year."

"I keep telling him it's time to get another dog," James said, "but he just won't listen to me."

"What kind of dog was he?" I asked.

"He was a German shepherd."

"Why don't you want another one?" I hadn't thought about it before, but now I realized the only thing that was missing from the ranch was a dog. "All ranches need dogs. Isn't it a federal law or something?"

The judge and James laughed. Mr. Hassler smiled, but it was a sad smile.

"I think it's a law, but they excuse you from it when there's a good chance the dog would outlive the rancher. I'm not getting any younger, and I don't know how long I'll keep the ranch. With my luck, I'd pick up a dog and he'd live for the next twelve years."

"You'll outlive us all, Dave," the judge chuckled.

"You need a dog," I told Mr. H.

"Good luck, Sean. I was telling him a few months before Abe died that he needed to get a new puppy. Abe would have been able to train him to take over the ranch."

"Well, that's what I've kept you for, James, so you'll know what to do with the ranch when I'm gone."

They all laughed, but I really didn't find anything amusing. Talking about Mr. Hassler dying and leaving his ranch to James didn't make me laugh at all.

We finished the meal with some carrot cake. As I went to do the dishes, the judge asked me to show him around the ranch.

"I haven't been here for a while. I'd like to see the place from a new person's point of view."

I looked instinctively at Mr. H. He dropped me a wink and barely moved his head forward. Yes, he was saying. You need to go.

"Sure," I said. "Just give me a few minutes to finish the dishes."

"C'mon, Frank, we'll leave these two pups to the dishes. Sean can meet us out by Knicker's stall."

James and I really didn't try to hurry and finish the dishes, and I was glad. I didn't know what the judge wanted. I didn't like judges or cops. They had never helped me before. Three times, the social workers had been out to see me because of the reports the cops and judges had filed. They made me lie. I had to tell them what a wonderful person my mother was. If I had ever told them the truth, they would have taken me away from everything I had ever known. I would rather stay where I knew the rules.

But Mr. H. trusted this judge. They seemed to be friends. Maybe I could trust him too.

When I got to Knicker's stall, the judge was waiting by himself.

"I hear you helped deliver this guy," he said as I walked up.

"Yeah."

"You ever deliver a baby before?"

"No." I grinned. "It was a real eye-opening experience."

He laughed. "I bet. But now you've got practical experience if you decide to become a vet."

"I guess so."

"Have you given much thought about what you want to be?"

I shook my head. "Haven't thought about it at all."

He didn't seem surprised or worried by my answer. "You've got plenty of time. Some kids decide what they want to be when they're in elementary school. I almost think that it limits them too much as they get older. It's important to explore things as you grow up." He cocked an eyebrow. "Legal things, that is. Exploring underage drinking and curfew violations are not necessarily good things to explore."

"I wasn't caught drinking," I began.

"You weren't caught," he interrupted, "because you left early. I'm sure if I called some of the kids caught at that party the sheriff busted the night you were brought in, I'd find several who would remember you being there."

I shifted from one foot to the other and concentrated on playing with Knicker's ears.

"But I'm not here to talk about that."

I looked at him. "Then what are you here to talk about?"

"I'm here because Dave thinks maybe you need someone to talk to. And also to get your statement about what happened last night."

I swallowed hard. "You mean between Mr. H. and my father?"

"Yep."

Knicker butted me. I had my back to the judge. I couldn't tell what he was thinking or feeling. I wouldn't have been able to anyway; I couldn't even tell what I was thinking or feeling.

"What do you need to know?"

"Well, I guess I'd like you to tell me in your own words what happened at the hospital last night."

"Actually, there's not much I can tell you. I wasn't there when he hit my father."

"Sean, how about you just start from the beginning. What happened last night after James left?"

So I told him. He didn't make many comments, just occasionally asked a question to make sure he understood what I meant.

"So your father gave you money, and then you tried to introduce him to Dave?"

"Yes."

"But your father wouldn't shake Dave's hand and that made you angry?"

"Yeah, it did. That plus the fact that he acted like he could just waltz in and be a part of my life again."

"When Dave was yelling at you in the field, how did you feel?"

"I felt like I had really let him down. Like I had maybe lost the chance to come back here."

"How did that make you feel?"

"It bugged me. Really bugged me."

"Did you ever feel like he was going to hurt you? Were you ever afraid he was going to hit you?"

"No. He wouldn't do that."

We left the stables and walked along the edge of the cornfield.

"Dave says he found you sleeping in Knicker's stall Wednesday morning."

"Yeah."

"Had you been there all night?"

"Yeah."

"Why?"

I told him about the fight with my mom.

"Explain to me again how you hurt your head."

"The second time she slammed me into the wall, my head hit a nail."

We had walked around the cornfield and were now approaching the paddock. Several horses were out grazing.

"Has your father been paying child support?" he asked abruptly.

"Oh yeah. He's too afraid not to."

"What do you mean?"

"His image is important to him. He doesn't want to look bad. The court said he had to pay us money, so he does. He believes in maintaining a perfect record. I'm sure he was there to pick up mom's hospital bill because he didn't want people thinking he was cold."

The judge started to say something, hesitated, and then said, "Let's come back to this later. This fight with your mother, was that the first one?"

I stopped and leaned against the fence, watching the pregnant mares graze. "No."

"How often does it happen?"

"I lose count. It's never the same from week to week. I can never tell what will set her off. I know it's not me, though."

"Does that make it easier to accept?"

"Sort of."

We walked and talked for nearly two hours. Finally, we started heading back to the house.

"Sean, how many other people know all the things you've told me today?"

"No one."

"Not even Dave?"

I shook my head, then added, "Well, he knows some of it, 'cause he was there. But he doesn't know all of it."

"Have you ever talked to any of your teachers about these things?"

I blinked in surprise. "Why would I?"

"Mrs. Walker, maybe, or Mr. Thomas?"

"Why would I?" I repeated.

"There are several teachers who care a great deal for you, Sean, even though you may not know it. Mrs. Walker caught me as I was going in to talk to your principal. She seemed especially concerned."

I was too surprised to say anything. I wanted to know what they had said about me, both the principal and Mrs. Walker, but I was afraid to ask.

"So if you haven't talked to anyone who knows you, why are you telling me, a complete stranger?"

I stopped and looked at him. "Because he asked me to."

"Dave?"

I nodded.

"He didn't ask you to tell him what happened the night you got the concussion?"

"Yeah, he did."

"So why are you telling me now?"

I kicked the dirt and turned in a half circle toward the dropping sun. "I want to make sure he doesn't get in trouble for what happened last night. He stuck his neck out for me. He shouldn't get his head chopped off for it."

"So you're doing this for him?"

"I guess."

"What do you think will happen now that you and I have talked, and you've told me all this?"

"I don't know."

"What do you want to happen? If you could pick your future, what would you do?"

"I don't know," I repeated.

"You must have some ideas. You've told me all the other stuff, why won't you tell me this?"

"Because then you might take it away."

He looked at me. "I can't take away what you don't have, Sean."

I didn't say anything.

"Well, how are you feeling about your dad now?"

"What do you mean?"

"What do you think about him?"

"I don't," I said flatly.

He raised his eyebrows and at that moment he looked a lot like Mr. H. He just waited.

"I…" I stopped, trying to gather my thoughts. I didn't know how to explain how I felt about my dad. "I guess I feel like he let me down."

"And how does that make you feel?"

"Angry." That I knew.

"Do you know why your dad left?"

"He said it was for a better job."

"Why?"

"So he could make more money."

The judge said slowly, "Well, he told me that he left for the better job in hopes that he could convince a judge to give him custody."

I stared at him. "You talked to my dad?"

"Yes," he said.

"My dad? You're sure you talked to my dad?"

"This morning."

I shook my head. "He's lying."

"Why would he do that?"

"Because he's just trying to look good. If he...I would...there's....Why would he want a worthless case like me back? And even if he did want custody, then why hasn't he come to see me for years? He hasn't even called!" I blurted out.

"Well," the judge said slowly, "he says that he's tried. He says at first when he called either no one answered, or when your mom did answer she hung up on him. When he finally figured out a time when you would be home, you hung up on him."

I kicked the dirt clod in the road.

"Further," the judge continued, "he says that he's tried to drop by several times in the last month since he moved back, but that no one's home when he does."

I opened my mouth to ask why he hadn't left a note for me, but then shut it again. I remembered, very clearly, coming home once with my mother and seeing her snatch a piece of paper from the door and crumple it up, swearing. I had always assumed it was a bill. Maybe it wasn't.

"Sean?"

I looked at him.

"Your dad would like the chance to see you and talk to you." The judge paused, probably trying to gauge my reaction. "He's dropping the charges against Dave. He said that he just lost his temper because he was hurt and jealous that you'd rather spend time with Dave. He said that after he got home he realized that he should be happy you found someone to stay with. But he'd still like a chance."

I looked at the judge. He stared back impassively, not trying to push me one way or the other, just laying out the options. I looked off to the stable.

"Does he want to come here, or does he want me to go see him?"

The judge smiled. "I'm sure he'd be happy with either. Do you think you could give him a call tonight? Maybe talk about a time when you would see him?"

"Maybe," I said, swallowing hard.

"Fair enough. Now will you tell me what you want your future to look like?"

"I still don't know."

"I'm offering you a choice, Sean."

"I don't have any choices," I said flatly. "I deal with what life gives me. It doesn't make much difference whether it comes from my parents, judges, or teachers, because it's never my choice. It's always somebody else's."

"Well, if you won't express your choices, maybe right now it's going to have to come from someone else. Let me tell you what I think your choices are." He sighed. "I think it's safe to say you won't be going back to your mother anytime soon. We'll just have to wait and see what terms you and your dad can work out; then we can figure out where you'll be living. And maybe you can talk Dave into one of his summer job positions. Other possibilities may come up; I just can't think of anything else right now." He stopped for a breath. "How does that sound?"

I thought about it for a minute. "Okay."

"Good." He smiled. "Now go get that colt used to being groomed. That was your chore for the afternoon, wasn't it?"

"Yes." I hesitated. "Thank you, Judge," I said awkwardly, holding out my hand.

He took it in a firm grasp. "Thank you, Sean, for taking the time to shed some light on the situation. And for being willing to give someone a second chance."

He headed back toward the house. I watched until I heard him yell "Dave!" before the door swung shut. Then I headed to the stable.

chapter thirteen

"**S**ean?"

I didn't look up from feeding Knicker. I was afraid he would yank the bottle right out of my hands if I did. "Yeah?" I asked absently.

"When he's done eating, just make a quick round of the stalls and pick up what needs picking up before you come in for dinner," Mr. H. said.

"Can't it wait till tomorrow?" I asked. My stomach had been gurgling all afternoon. I really didn't want to lose my appetite now.

"Sean," Mr. H. sighed. "One thing you've got to learn about this ranch is that things need to be done when they need to be done. Not after they need to be done. The animals depend on us. How would you like to spend the night in your room if it was full of—"

"All right, all right." I could see where this conversation was going and it really wasn't doing anything for me visually. "I'll do one last pick-up round before I come in for dinner. By the way," I added casually, "what's for dinner?"

"I don't know. What are you making?"

Now I did look up. "Huh?"

"Now that you're staying here for a while, you'll have to help out with the cooking on a regular basis. And tonight's as good a night as any to get started."

I rolled my eyes and tried to fight back the angry words. He was taking advantage of me. "Does all this count for my hours?" I asked, trying, but failing, to keep the frustration out of my voice.

"Of course," he said easily. "It all counts."

He left, probably going to sit and chew on his pipe, and listen to the radio in his easy chair. The fact that I had three chores to complete before I could sit and relax kept buzzing around in my head. And even then, the angry wasp in my ear whispered, you won't be allowed to relax! Oh, no, he'll make sure you go up and spend a few hours doing homework!

Knicker butted my chest and whinnied at me. I absently pulled on his ear, scratching the side of his stubby mane. I took a deep breath. Might as well get started. As Mr. H. had pointed out on my first happy day here, the stalls aren't going to muck themselves. I found the shovel with no problem, and I also discovered a beat-up wheelbarrow that seemed accustomed to carrying manure around.

As I made the round of the stalls, my anger toward Mr. H. began to fade. Very few of the stalls had anything in them. I guess that's why he hadn't felt bad giving me this last job tonight. That might also explain why the paddock takes so long to clean.

I had actually started to whistle a little when I hit the third stall that had a pile in it. I swung the stall door open and then froze.

It was Manda. I hadn't seen her since the first night. I hadn't even thought about her, really, except when James had suggested trying to put Knicker back with her.

She turned her head slowly, arrogantly. She was a pretty mare, probably one of the prettiest there, but I couldn't stand the sight of her. Her red coat glistened like satin, and her long mane and tail hung as elegantly as if someone had brushed them for hours. Mr. H. had described her as having good lines. I didn't know much about horses, but I had to admire her graceful, slender legs and the fine cut of her face.

She swished her tail, attitude in every inch of her body. Her eyes, while they were the same deep dark brown as Knicker's, were cold and uncaring. There was no spark of liveliness in them. She couldn't care less that I was there, any more than she cared that her son was now dependent on strangers for his life.

I took a deep breath and shifted the shovel in my hands. My fingers began to tingle, and I realized I had been gripping the handle so hard my knuckles were white. I also had raised the shovel as if I intended to strike her with it.

This was not good. *Screw it,* I said to myself. *Let her sleep with crap in her stall. It's no less than she deserves.*

I shut the stall door. She flicked an ear back, forward again, and then turned back to her pile of hay.

I stood there for a few minutes, just staring at her. I wanted her to feel my anger, wanted her to know how much I really despised her. She never looked up at me again, only swished her tail once or twice, slowly. But I knew that she knew I was there. She was just showing me how little she cared, how little I mattered.

I turned and completed my round of the barn in fifteen minutes. It took me a while because I stopped to pet the horses whose stalls had "gifts" in them. They were all pretty interested in me. Two bobbed their heads up and down over their doors as they saw me coming, and were actually kind of a pain as I was trying to shovel because they kept getting in my way. One of them was kind of bashful, but after I introduced myself, he allowed me to pet him, and snorted when I turned to leave.

I had to walk back past Manda's stall to take the shovel and wheelbarrow back. She was still in the corner, one leg bent so her horseshoe reflected the light. I hesitated. If I went in tonight without cleaning all of the stalls, would anyone really be able to tell? It was, after all, just one stall. And surely some of the other horses would have to take a dump before the morning, so who's to say her stall wasn't clean when I checked it?

I sighed. I'd know, and for the first time in my life, that was enough. I knew that when Mr. H. asked me this evening if the stalls were clean that I wouldn't be able to lie. Well, I could probably say the words, but he'd know I was lying. I don't know how he'd know, but he would. And he'd throw a guilt trip on me. He'd taken me in. Sure, he'd worked my butt off, but that's what comes with community service. But he had done more than just make me work, and I knew it.

Maybe I'll get lucky, I thought, grabbing the handle and opening the stall door. *Maybe she'll just continue to ignore me. I can get the load in one shovelful and get out of here.* So far that seemed reasonable; she didn't even turn her head when I opened the door.

I quickly stepped inside, trying to be quiet, willing myself to become invisible. I loaded the shovel, but she had left quite a pile, and I would have to come back.

I stepped out into the corridor and dropped the load into the wheelbarrow. When I turned around, I flinched.

Apparently she could move quickly and quietly, too. She was already walking through the door. I hadn't even heard the straw rustle when she moved.

"Where do you think you're going?" I demanded. I stepped forward, intending to just shove her chest and get her to back into the stall.

She laid her ears back against her head and bared her teeth at me.

Something inside me snapped. I didn't feel it right away, but something inside me really snapped.

I lifted the shovel. She shook her head back and forth, teeth still bared. I could just see her thinking that people had tried to scare her with shovels before, so it really wasn't going to work this time. Her eyes had an evil glint to them, and I was reminded of how she had ripped Mr. Hassler's shirt and arm the night Knicker was born.

I turned the shovel so I was holding it above the blade with the handle over my shoulder like a bat. I had no intention of just trying to scare her.

She snaked her head in, going for my thigh. The handle arced up and over, and I brought it down squarely on her muzzle. I stopped putting force into it about halfway through the arc, allowing gravity to finish the job.

I didn't know what kind of reaction to expect, but the last one I was looking for was a renewed attack on her part. She lunged for me, I wasn't ready for it, and she knocked me clear into the next stall. In the process, she used her teeth to try to remove my shoulder. I couldn't believe how much it hurt.

I jumped up, never really feeling myself hit the ground. I grabbed the shovel, this time just at the top of the handle, and brought the shovel up as hard as I could into the middle of her rib cage. I hit her with the broadside of the shovel, not with the edge, and I felt rather than heard a solid thunk as it connected with her.

She gave a startled grunt with a whooshing sound, like I had knocked all of the air out of her. It stopped the forward motion of her head. I was relieved, because it had looked like she was getting ready to take a large chunk out of my leg.

Manda dropped her head down close to the ground and began to shake all over. Whether from fear or rage, I couldn't tell.

I waited for a minute, the anger in me slowly boiling over. "Go on! Get back in your stall!" I had started out in a moderate tone, but by the end I was shouting.

Her head came up slowly, nostrils flaring and ears pinned back again. This time, though, I wasn't playing defensively.

I brought the shovel across the front of me and gave all of my strength to a backhand swing to her chest. She jerked her head up even higher, and reared up on her hind legs. I swung again, hitting the soft underside of her belly. She came down quickly.

I started thrusting the shovel at her like a huge sword. When Manda backed into the stall wall, she hesitated and began to turn slightly.

"No way," I panted, "not in this lifetime. You're not getting out of here. Get back, you rotten tramp! *Get back!*" I hollered, still using the shovel like a lance.

Manda backed into the stall, no hesitation or arrogance anymore. She was beat and she knew it. I knew it too, but I kept after her, kept driving her back in her stall until she was huddled in the farthest corner, trying to escape the blows of the shovel.

I lost all track of time. It could have been three seconds, three minutes, three hours. I hit her again and again with the shovel handle. I yelled at her, cursed her, cried because of her.

Steel arms caught mine in the middle of one of my weakening swings. A vise of muscle came around my midsection and pinned both arms to my side.

"Sweet Jesus," I heard Mr. Hassler whisper from the corridor behind me.

I stopped fighting. I blinked twice, trying to clear my sight. There was no way that I saw what I thought I saw.

Manda was down in the straw, bleeding from several places. Her body was shaking violently. The grip around me was continuing to tighten. I yelped involuntarily.

"Let him go," Mr. Hassler told James. "Sean, come inside the house. We'll need to call a couple of doctors."

For a minute or two, it didn't seem that James was going to listen to Mr. H. It seemed that he was just going to continue squeezing the breath out of me until I fell to the ground as Manda had. *When had that happened? I wondered. I don't remember seeing her fall.*

Slowly, ever so slowly, James released me. I turned and stumbled as I went to the door. When I reached out to grab the wall for support, I bit back a cry. The sharp pain in my shoulder reminded me of what Manda had done to me.

I kept my eyes down. I couldn't look at Mr. Hassler. I knew there would be fire in his eyes; I knew I had crossed an unforgivable line. But I didn't remember crossing it. I didn't mean to hurt her. I had just wanted to get her back into her stall. If she had gotten out, I would have been in trouble, so I tried to put her back. But then...she had...I...

Blindly, I followed Mr. Hassler through the barn. Knicker nickered when we passed his stall, but I couldn't look at him. Just thinking about him and Manda made me sick. The cold air hit me, stinging my face, sending new needles of pain into the open wound on my shoulder. I stopped just outside the door and threw up.

I don't even remember walking up to the house.

The bright fluorescent glare of the kitchen lights made me squint. I sank down into the nearest chair, too drained to move. I felt stunned. And the stupid thing was, it was all my fault.

Mr. Hassler picked up the phone and after he finished dialing, he took the phone to the sink. "Hello, Doc, it's Dave...." He pulled a towel out of a drawer. "Yeah, I know I'm becoming a regular.... Need you to come out here, as soon as you can.... No, not another delivery, Casper's still holding on.... I'd rather wait till you get out here.... Well, it could probably wait till tomorrow, but I'd rather not..." He finished running warm water over the towel and was wringing it out. "I really appreciate it, Doc.... Just go straight to the barn. I've got to run into town.... No, you know I wouldn't leave my horses if I could help it, but I've got to run Sean into the hospital.... Yeah, I'll talk to you tomorrow.... Thanks again." He hung up and immediately began dialing the phone again.

He looked at me quickly. "Take your shirt off," he whispered. "Steve, Dave Hassler.... Sorry to bother you so late, but I was wondering if you could meet me at the hospital in a few minutes.... Hold on a second."

I was struggling to get my T-shirt off. My shoulder was burning and throbbing and too stiff to move. Mr. H. grabbed some scissors and in one quick motion cut the shirt in half down the front and then started to help me take it off like a jacket.

"Steve? No, it's not for me...." Mr. Hassler gently pulled the shirt away from the wound. "Yes, young Sean needs your assistance again. I don't think it's too serious, but it will take a few stitches at least." I was shaking my head, but Mr. H. was ignoring me. "This time you can talk to him, and that will save you the follow-up trip back out here tomorrow.... Well, yeah, I guess you will have to do another follow-up trip anyway, but you can save it for later.... Great, we'll see you in fifteen minutes."

Mr. Hassler hung up the phone and started out of the kitchen. He turned and called to me, "Put that towel on your shoulder and use as much pressure on it as you can stand. I'll be right back."

"I don't need to go to the hospital," I muttered, biting my lip as I placed the towel on my shoulder. I stood up and held on to the table for a minute before making my way across the kitchen to the front door.

Mr. H. had amazing hearing. "Yes, you do, Sean. My guess is you'll get close to twenty stitches." He was coming down the stairs, putting his wallet in his pocket and carrying the jacket I had been using. He swung the jacket across my shoulders and put his hand on my back to guide me out the door.

We got in the truck, and I sat stiffly, waiting for him to rip into me. He was silent. I stole a glance at him. He was concentrating on something more than the driving, but he didn't really look angry. Concerned and anxious, yes, but angry and tense, no.

My mind was whirling. "Aren't you going to say anything?" I finally asked.

He glanced over at me. "What would you like me to say?"

I stared at him. He was serious. He wasn't mocking me or being sarcastic. "Aren't you going to yell at me, or tell me what a jerk I am...or...or let me have it somehow?" I was at a loss for words.

"Do you think you're a jerk?" he asked softly.

I stared at the dashboard. Jerk didn't even come close to what I was thinking I was.

"Is there a reason I should yell at you?"

"Weren't you the one who was just in the barn with me?" I asked in disbelief.

"Yes," he said easily. "Is there a reason I should yell at you?"

"I don't believe this," I said, shaking my head. "I was totally out of control. I beat the crap out of a defenseless animal. It was awful..." I trailed off. I couldn't describe it.

We sat in the silence for a few more minutes. "Don't you have anything to say to me?" I asked again.

"Sean, I have lots of things to say to you. I don't, however, have anything to yell about."

"I don't understand," I said.

He sighed. "I shouldn't have left you alone with Manda. That was my mistake. Not only is she a very temperamental and occasionally violent mare, I also knew that you had some resentment toward her. I had no idea it was that extreme, but I was aware of it. It was an oversight on my part, but you and Manda are the ones who are paying for it right now."

I'm pretty sure that hinges on my mouth broke at this time, because I had a hard time picking my jaw up off the ground. "You weren't there. It was my fault, not yours. I…God, I don't even know how to explain what I did." I leaned my head back and shut my eyes. The pain in my shoulder was getting worse.

"I think I might know how to explain it, Sean."

I looked over at him. "How would you know?"

He shrugged a little. "I said I might, I didn't say for sure that I knew. I would know if you would just talk to me."

"I talk to you," I said a little defensively.

"Yes, you talk to me, but not about the important things in your life. Not about you. Not about your family." He paused, looking at me out of the corner of his eye. "I think," he began carefully, "that you did what you did to Manda because of what she did to Knicker, and because of what your mother did to you."

I felt myself tensing all over. I forced myself to breathe slowly, trying to relax and not explode again.

Mr. H. cleared his throat roughly. "Frank related some parts of your conversation this afternoon. Not all of it," he added quickly, "just the parts that he thought I needed to know. And," his voice dropped to a whisper, "I told him I suspected your mother might be abusive."

Again, silence filled the cab.

We pulled into the hospital parking lot. Neither of us spoke as he found a spot and turned off the engine. As I reached out to open the door, he stopped me by placing his hand gently on my uninjured shoulder.

"Sean, you'll be seeing Dr. Morris tonight. He's the one who saw you the other morning. You were unconscious at the time, so he didn't get to talk to you. He's pretty concerned about how you received your injuries." Mr. H.'s steady gaze never faltered, and his voice never changed. "He's going to ask you a lot of questions about your mom. He's also required by law to report any suspected child abuse. I know you have a hard time talking to people.

Dr. Morris is a good man who would like to help you. I hope you can talk to him, even if you can't talk to me."

I wanted to put my head on Mr. H.'s shoulder right then and just bawl out my entire story. But he was already turning around, letting himself out of the truck, and I had to open my door and follow him into the hospital.

I took a deep breath, feeling the cold air fill my lungs and clear my head. I looked up to the stars, watching them sparkle, and then I hurried after Mr. Hassler into the hospital lights.

Dr. Morris turned out to be a pretty nice doctor. Maybe it was just because he seemed so young. Every other doctor I've ever seen looked to be about fifteen years past retirement, but Dr. Morris couldn't have been more than forty.

"Hi, Sean."

"Hi, Dr. Morris."

"You probably don't remember, but we've met once before."

I tried to smile. "So I hear."

He turned to Mr. H. "I'll clean and stitch him, and I think a tetanus shot is in order tonight. All that will probably take about twenty minutes. So, how 'bout you come back in, oh, say, forty minutes or so? Give us a little time for a chat."

Mr. H. nodded and turned to leave the room.

"Wait!"

They both turned to me quickly, like they thought something was wrong. I didn't realize how panicky I sounded. I tried to moderate my voice. "I'd rather you stay here, if you don't mind."

Mr. H. grinned. "Don't mind at all. But are you sure you don't want me to go get you a soda or a chocolate bar?"

"No, I'm fine."

I ended up getting fifteen stitches and a tetanus shot, but they weren't as painful as having to repeat my story for the second time in one day. After years of having no one to really talk to, having so many people act interested started to freak me out. I really didn't want to talk, and I know I snapped at Dr. Morris more than I should have, but he was pretty understanding about it. I was glad he let Mr. Hassler stay with me. That way I wouldn't have to tell my story again.

chapter fourteen

The rest of Saturday night passed in a whirl. Dinner started out pretty quiet. I didn't feel much like talking, and I could tell James was still upset about what I had done to Manda. All I wanted to do was go hide in bed, but Mr. H. made James and me cook dinner together in the kitchen. It was awful at first, but then James began to relax a little. By the time we sat down to eat, things were almost normal.

We talked about all sorts of things that evening. James and I argued about who we thought would win the Super Bowl. Mr. H. said he didn't care because the only real American sport was baseball. We agreed that all sports had become too commercial. James mentioned a new movie he had seen the preview for, and we talked about our favorite actors and types of movies. Mr. Hassler just sat and listened to us; I got the feeling he was trying really hard not to laugh at us.

Mr. H. and James talked about the harvest for a while. I listened even though not much of what they said made any sense to me; most of the work had been done before I was there. But I listened because I wanted to know about the ranch. I wasn't involved in its past, but I wanted to be involved in its future.

I wanted to ask Mr. H. if the judge had asked him about letting me stay on a semipermanent basis, but I was afraid of the answer I might get. So instead I asked about working on the ranch during the summer camp.

"Well," he drawled. "I think that would be a possibility. I hire six wranglers each summer, and they've always got first choice to return if they want to. But it seems to me that two or three of them from last year said that they might not be returning next summer."

James agreed, his eyes laughing at me.

"What do you mean by 'wrangler'?"

"Stable hand," he replied. "Guide for the rides."

"Oh," I said quietly.

"What's wrong?" James asked.

"I could help in the stable, but I don't know how to ride." I was trying to hide my panic, but I don't think I did a good job.

"Hmmm, that could be a problem," Mr. H. said, rubbing his cheek thoughtfully.

"Yeah," James agreed, "I think it might even be a big problem."

I could tell he was just kidding me, but I really didn't feel like laughing. I should have known that you'd have to be able to ride in order to get a job at a ranch.

"The other thing my wranglers do is cook. But in the summer I've got twenty kids here a week. You'd have a lot of learning to do in the kitchen."

"No offense, Sean, but from what I've seen so far, I think trying to teach you to cook for twenty kids and all the wranglers would be a lost cause. Even though we would probably keep the fire department in business," James said with a laugh.

"Of course," Mr. Hassler continued, still thinking, "we are talking about next summer."

"And summer is still months away," James added.

"How long do you reckon it takes a man to learn how to ride?" Mr. H. asked James.

"I don't know," James said, shaking his head. "It would depend on how badly he wanted to learn and how much time he was willing to spend on it. And," he added with an evil grin, "it would depend on how sore he's willing to get."

I looked from one man to the other. "Are you saying maybe I could learn to ride in time to get a job?"

"It's a definite possibility, Sean—"

"A better possibility than you cooking," James interrupted, chuckling. Mr. H. shot him a look and he shut up.

Mr. H. continued in a serious tone of voice. "But let's work on one day at a time, okay? Come springtime, you may have decided you're tired of listening to an old man."

"I won't be," I said confidently. "Can I have some more hot fudge?"

That Sunday morning was the first one in my memory where I got up early and really didn't mind it. I knew that Knicker was depending on me for breakfast, and a lot of other horses, cows, and llamas were, too. And, in a not-so-evident way, so was Mr. Hassler.

I spent the first hour mucking out the horse stalls, and then forty-five minutes on the cow and llama barn. My shoulder slowed me down a little, but I was determined to finish. I knew if I couldn't do one chore, then I wouldn't be allowed to do the others. I worked with Knicker some more. I was very proud of him. I could come up and just slip the halter over his face, and he didn't try to run or fight me at all. He was also pretty good about being groomed. At least, he was good for the first five or ten minutes. Then he'd get antsy and wouldn't stay still for me. He'd much rather play tag.

Mr. H. told me that we should start trying to get him to eat small amounts of warm oats mashed in milk that evening and then try to increase the amount each day until he was completely off the bottle. He said it wouldn't feel as natural to Knicker as bottle feeding, but it would be a little more practical.

Knicker was acting more and more like a puppy around me. It worried me a little, but I also kind of liked it. Besides, I didn't really know how a foal was supposed to act anyway.

Mr. Hassler had sandwiches ready for James and me when we came in for lunch, and then he had an extra surprise.

"Why don't you two take the afternoon off and go catch that movie y'all were talking about last night?"

James and I looked at each other. "But, I was…" I began.

James reached across the table quickly and covered my mouth with his hand. "Sean, you ain't been here long enough to understand, but when Boss lets you take the day off, you take it with no questions asked," he said, grinning.

"Okay," I said with a shrug. "Can I just stay and take my afternoon off with Knicker?"

James shook his head vehemently. "If you're around, he'll find something for you to do. We get the day off, we take it, and we take it to town. Those are the basic survival rules you need to know."

"Okay, okay, sorry," I said, getting up to start the dishes.

"However," I heard James say, "I think you need to go with us, Boss."

Mr. H. just laughed all the way out of the kitchen.

"Well, you tried," I told him.

"Yeah, it was the least I could do when he gave us a holiday. He also told me that the first show starts in half an hour, so we better get cranking."

"Does that seem strange to you?"

"What do you mean?"

"Well, it kind of feels like he's trying to get us out of the house. Like he wants to get rid of us."

"Naw," James said. "This is just something he does every once in a while. We were talking about movies the last couple of nights, and he probably decided this morning to look up show times and then give us this surprise. It doesn't mean anything."

"Okay," I said, but I wasn't entirely convinced.

As we headed into town, an idea entered my mind and just wouldn't let go. I had to see if it was possible.

"Hey, James, can we swing by my house real quick?"

"Why?"

"I need to get a phone number. And my math book. I should try to do the next few pages before I go back tomorrow. Mr. Javerneal is the pickiest teacher about accepting late work."

James looked at me kind of funny, but he really couldn't argue because he knew Mr. H. wanted me doing homework.

There was a note stuck to the front door and I grabbed it on my way inside. My heart skipped a beat, as I briefly considered that the note might be from my father. It was from Lee. I skimmed it on the way to the phone. Some gibberish about Rick looking for me to even the score. I dropped the note in the trash, and made the phone call as quickly as I could. I got the answer I wanted, and I whistled all the way back to my room.

I picked up my math book, and then just on a hunch, checked two of my mother's hiding places for cash. I struck out on the first one, but found nearly forty-five dollars in the second. It made me feel scuzzy to sink to her level, but it couldn't be avoided. I no longer just wanted to do this; I needed to.

The movie was great. I've always enjoyed science fiction movies, and this one was better than most. I tried to pay for the movie, but James said the Boss had slipped him some cash to pay for both of us.

After the movie, he dragged me into a cheap department store.

"I know this place probably doesn't have all the fashion stuff that you like," he started, but then a hand came down hard on my bad shoulder and I yelled out.

I turned around and Mrs. Walker was staring at me, wide-eyed.

"My God, Sean, I didn't mean to scare you that badly!"

"You didn't," I said, gingerly touching my shoulder. I explained what had happened as quickly as I could. I didn't quite tell her everything that I had done to Manda, but that was more because I didn't want to think about it.

"I'm so sorry!" she said when I had explained. "I didn't mean to hurt you. I just wanted to say hi and see how you're doing."

"Jeez," I said. "I'm seeing more of you this week than I do when I'm in school."

"Now, I know you're not complaining," she said with a grin. "How has your week been?"

"Fine," I said. I always felt awkward seeing teachers outside of the school. They just didn't seem natural anywhere else.

"Is Knicker still doing all right?"

"Yeah," I said, smiling in spite of myself. "He's doing real well."

"I'm glad to hear it. You'll be back tomorrow, right?"

"Right. And I'll be in class, not in in-house."

"Good," she said. "We need you back in class." She paused for a moment. "Do you have your paper done?"

"Almost," I said, stretching the truth a bit. "We better get going. See ya tomorrow morning."

"Okay," she smiled. "Tell Dave I said hello. I'll try to drop by again soon."

I laughed and shook my head. It was cool in a way that she cared, but really, enough was enough.

We said good-bye, and James continued what he had started saying earlier. "Boss thinks you need some new jeans. He thinks you're going to wear yours out pretty soon, working like you have been. So he said I'm supposed to rig you out in a uniform. Something that will be comfortable for work. Blue jeans, maybe a flannel shirt, some T-shirts, and a sturdy pair of shoes."

"Oh, hey, let's just go back to my house. I can pick up some more clothes."

James looked at me. "Can you make them look like we just bought them for you?"

I thought about my wardrobe. The newest thing I had was a T-shirt from a concert six months ago.

"He wants to do this, Sean," he insisted. "He knows how hard you've been working. He expects you to keep it up."

I still wasn't sure.

"Look, you're not going to have to wear this stuff to school, if you're worried about how you'll look. You'll just have some warm work clothes."

I ended up with two pairs of jeans, three T-shirts, and a couple of flannel shirts. I could fit the mountain man look now with no problem. Except that wasn't my style.

We started home.

"Hey, James," I said as casually as I could, "do you mind making one more stop?"

He looked at me out of the corner of his eye. "What kind of stop?"

"Well, I'd kind of like to get something for Mr. Hassler—that's what I made the phone call for—and it will be a quick stop, I promise," I said in a rush.

He laughed. "Well, that's all fine with me, Sean, but you didn't tell me what we're stopping for."

Oh, great, I thought. *What am I supposed to tell him now?* I was afraid he'd say no, but if I didn't tell him anything, I was sure he wouldn't stop.

"My friend's dog had puppies," I said in a bored tone, trying not to sound too hung up on the idea, "and they're selling them for ten bucks each. I thought if I gave him a puppy, he couldn't turn it down."

"Oh, Sean," he groaned. "You've put me in one heck of a pickle."

He thought about it for a few minutes, and I could tell he really didn't know which way to go. "You said the other night that you think he should get another dog," I argued.

"Yeah, but it's also not the kind of thing you should force on a person. Getting a pet is a responsibility you should take on yourself, not a decision someone else should make for you."

"Well," I said, thinking quickly, "if he really doesn't want it, we'll take it back, or find it another home for it."

"Sean, he'll blame me for this."

"No, he won't."

"Yes, he will. I'm the one driving, remember?"

"Okay, so we'll say I ran away. And then I'll walk up the drive with the puppy."

"He'll blame me for letting you get away."

"Please, James, I want to get him a puppy."

He sighed and looked at me. "You do know how to make things difficult."

I just sat there and kept my mouth shut.

Finally he said, "Well, where do I go?"

When we pulled up to the house, not only did we have the puppy, we also had a twenty-pound bag of food, three chew toys, a box of puppy treats, and a sleeping basket. The puppy was a shepherd-Labrador mix. He was a soft, fuzzy ball, black from the tip of his nose to the tip of his tail, with just a small white spot on his right front paw.

I hesitated outside the front door. James had refused to come in with me.

"Depending on how he takes this," he had said with a strange grin, "this is either your battle to fight or your gift to give. Either way, I'm staying out of it."

"Chicken," I muttered at him.

"Yes," he had agreed. "I like chickens. The wild ones live longer than most birds."

I slipped silently into the house. Mr. H. was sitting in his favorite chair, pipe nearly falling out of his mouth. He had the paper spread out in front of him, but his eyes were closed.

I didn't know what to say, so I knelt down and let the puppy go. He went off exploring, looking for new scents and people. When he discovered Mr. H., he cocked his head to one side and stared at him.

Suddenly, he burst into a series of puppy yips. I don't know who jumped higher, me or Mr. Hassler.

"What the—" he yelped, throwing the paper up and over everything, including the puppy. His pipe fell out of his mouth and bounced on the floor, smacking the puppy on the nose. The puppy began whimpering and immediately made a puddle on the floor. "Where in blazes did you come from?" Mr. H. shouted, grabbing the newspaper to mop up the puddle.

I stuck my head into the room. "Um, hello! We're back," I said, doing my best to smile.

"Did you forget to drop something off at the pound, or are we having a really fresh Chinese delicacy for supper?"

The puppy may not have understood what was said, but he certainly understood the tone. He slunk over to me with his tail tucked firmly between his back legs. I knew exactly how he felt.

I charged on ahead anyway. "You need a puppy. So I got one for you."

"I told you, Sean, I'm too old for a puppy. Why don't you listen to what people say?"

"I heard what you said, but I didn't think you meant it."

He looked at me. It's really amazing what can be said without any words.

"Well, okay, I knew you meant it, but I thought maybe he could change your mind," I said, nodding toward the puppy.

"Why does my mind need changing?"

"I'm sorry. It's just that my friend's dog had puppies, and after the conversation the other night, I thought I could help both of you out. Find a home for one of his puppies, and a companion and fox chaser for you."

"He can't stay."

"Okay. I'll find him another home."

"Why don't you and James take him back to his mama?"

"I can't do that! It'd be like lying to my friend. I'll just find another home for the puppy."

"And just how long do you think that will take? A day? A week? A year?"

"I don't know," I admitted. "But I'll find him a home, I swear. Anyway," I added, "he'll go when I go."

"I can't believe this," Mr. H. growled. "Well, if he's here for a little while, you and James might as well go get him some food and line a box for his bed."

On cue, James stepped through the front door, loaded down with the puppy supplies we had purchased. When Mr. H. cleared his throat, James looked up at him, and then looked away quickly. I hurried forward to help him. The puppy nearly tripped me, still trying to stay safely behind my legs.

"Oh, Lord, help me keep these three young pups in line," I heard Mr. H. mutter as he left the room.

That evening, Mr. H. dug out a typewriter for me to use. It was so old I could barely recognize what it was. He sat me at the kitchen table, gave me a fresh pack of paper and a dictionary, and told me he didn't want me leaving the kitchen until I was done with my paper. Then he left for his favorite chair in the living room.

I followed him a few minutes later.

"I know you're not done yet," he said around his pipe without looking up.

"No, I can't start."

Now he did look up. "Why not?"

"I don't know how to plug it in."

"You don't plug it in," he said, looking at me like I was from an unknown planet.

"Then how does it turn on?"

He folded the paper on his lap. "You don't turn it on."

"Huh?"

"It's manual!" He put his hands up to his forehead as if he were in great pain. "The harder you strike the keys, the darker the letters."

I turned to go try this "manual" typewriter.

"And you can't just delete your errors," he called over his shoulder. "So be careful."

I will never complain about computers again. My fingers kept slipping in between the keys and it hurt. Plus, I kept messing up. I started the paper over at least eight times before I gave up on neatness. I decided to just cross out the mistakes.

I finished a sloppy copy of my paper but was too frustrated to try to make it any neater. I went back through my journal entries, adding and changing things. We were supposed to make daily entries, but I hoped Mrs. Walker wouldn't know the difference. Mr. Hassler came in and told me to take a fifteen-minute study break at eight-thirty.

"No, that's okay," I said. "I'll just keep going," I figured that since he didn't have a TV I might as well just get the work done.

"It's a good idea to take a little break, it keeps the mind going and gives the fingers a rest." He stopped for a second. "Maybe this would be a good time to reach your father."

I looked at him, but he was digging in the cupboard for the instant coffee. I pushed my chair back and headed to the living room, where I simply stared at the phone for a good five minutes. What was I going to say? I knew I had to call him, but I promised myself that if the bimbo answered I would hang up again. I picked up the phone and slowly dialed the number.

"Hello?"

"Hi, Dad. It's me, Sean," I said in a rush.

"Hi, Sean," he replied.

I could hear the hesitation in his voice. Neither of us said anything. It was awful. Finally I just blurted out, "I'm sorry," and for no apparent reason, I felt a tear slip down my cheek.

He let out a long sigh. "No, Sean, I'm the one who's sorry. I'm sorrier than you'll ever know. I'm sorry for everything."

"No, Dad," I said. For some weird reason I couldn't stand to hear him say that. "It's no big deal. I was just being a brat."

"And I was being pretty pushy."

"Hey, can we stop apologizing now?" I asked.

He chuckled a little. "Sure." He paused briefly. "Are you at home?"

"No," I said. "I'm at Mr. Hassler's. He's got this great ranch here."

"I see." Another pause. "What have you been up to lately?"

I squirmed. "I'm still doing my community service hours."

"I see," Dad repeated slowly.

"I helped deliver a foal my first night here," I said, and then I could have kicked myself. I sounded like a little kid, trying to show off.

"Is that so? What's his name?"

"Knicker." Even I could hear the pride in my voice.

"I see."

That awkward silence fell again. This time I didn't know what else to say.

"Um, Sean," Dad said, clearing his throat, "could we get together sometime this week? I think we've got a lot to talk about."

"Yeah," I said. "I guess so."

"Is there a day that works well for you?"

I couldn't believe he didn't just tell me when we'd be meeting. "Um, I don't really think it matters."

"How about after school tomorrow?"

"Could we make it Tuesday?" I asked.

"Sure," he said. I felt like a jerk, but at the same time I liked hearing the uncertainty in his voice.

"Just because I'll have a lot of makeup work to do tomorrow night," I explained.

"I'm glad to hear you're worried about your schoolwork. Tuesday sounds fine. Can I pick you up at your mom's around three?"

"As long as you'll drop me off here," I said.

"Is that all right with Mr., um, Hackler?"

"Hassler," I corrected. "Yes."

"Then I guess it's all right with me," he said, but I could tell he didn't like it. It made me feel good to know he didn't like it, but I wasn't going to change my plans just because it bothered him. He hadn't done much in the last few years, so how was I to know if he was really going to change this time?

"Well, I'll see you Tuesday," I said, wanting to end the conversation.

"Yeah, Sean, see you Tuesday." He hesitated. "Take care of yourself, okay?"

"Yeah, Dad. You, too." And I hung up the phone.

When I returned to the kitchen, there was a tall glass of milk and a plate of cookies waiting for me. Mr. Hassler wasn't in sight. I laughed, but this time it wasn't because I thought it was stupid.

I managed to complete a fairly neat copy around ten. I went to show it to Mr. H., because he had been giving me so much grief about it. He was still in the easy chair, but the pipe had fallen out of his mouth, and he was snoring lightly. The puppy was curled up in a ball at his feet.

I started to back out of the room when a thought struck me. I almost didn't have the courage to do it, but I thought to myself, *what goes around comes around*, and did it anyway.

There was an old blanket folded on the corner of the couch, and I spread it out over him, doing my best not to wake him. The puppy woke up, so I picked him up and took him outside for a few minutes so he could do his thing. Then I turned the light off in the living room as I snuck quietly upstairs with the puppy.

chapter fifteen

oing back to school was like being shoved into a coffin. It was
strange that it bothered me so much. I mean, I had been out of
school before—for spring break, summer vacations, and the
occasional suspension—but going back had never bothered me so much
before.

I felt like I hadn't seen my friends in years. Talking to them was strange.
All they wanted to talk about were the parties from last week, the new
couples, and who was now on probation. Apparently the big news was that
Rick had bought some drugs and was trying to sell them around school.
None of that seemed real to me anymore. I felt out of touch.

But what I had been through—well, that was something unreal for them.
I tried to talk to Mike about it, but I gave up because I had no idea how to
explain what had happened to me, what it meant to me. So all I ended up
saying was that I was serving my time on a ranch, and that I had helped
deliver a baby horse. Even saying that was too much. Mike started razzing
me and even went so far as trying to make a horse sound. He didn't do it
very well, but he did it loud enough to attract some attention.

"Yo, man, where's your pet dog?" an angry voice called out from across
the hall.

Mike glared at Rick. "What dog?"

"I dunno. It sounds like you ate one and he's trying to get out."

Some of the kids who had started to gather around us giggled nervously.

Then Rick turned his attention back to me. "Yo, Farm Boy, we still got
some things to settle."

I just looked at him, using my best imitation of Mr. Hassler's bored stare.

The bell rang, and I could see two teachers approaching the group
forming around us. I shrugged. "Whenever, man. Ain't no thing to me." I
turned and started to walk away.

Rick grabbed my sore shoulder. I didn't let him know how much it hurt. "Oh, but it is, man, it is," he snarled.

"Let's get going to class, guys. Come on, you're going to be late to first period," Mr. Darrell said behind Rick.

I shook Rick's hand off my shoulder and followed Lee to math.

During the morning classes, I was quiet. I ignored people if their conversation bored me. Most of the time it did, because it seemed everyone was convinced that Rick and I still had something to settle. At least, that's what he had told everyone.

A few people asked about my community service and wanted to know if I had had to pay a fine, too. The guys and some of the girls were interested in case they were ever in my shoes. Most of the girls, though, just looked like they were scared of me.

By third hour, I had started talking a little more. I was careful about the way I answered questions about my week, but as long as this was causing such a stir, I thought I might as well enjoy it. No need to come off looking like a nerd.

The only time I really felt normal again was in Mrs. Walker's class. The other teachers had glanced at me indifferently. I knew most of them didn't believe I would ever do the makeup work, so they didn't take much time to explain how to do it. But Mrs. Walker knew that I had done my work and that I would do the rest of my assignments. She didn't think it was because I wanted to; she thought it was because I was staying with Mr. Hassler.

As soon as I sat down, she asked me, "Do you have your hero paper, Sean?"

"Yep," I said, "right here."

And I opened my book—to a series of math problems. I couldn't believe it.

"Sean?" She was waiting.

"I, uh, I left it in my locker," I stuttered.

Mrs. Walker sighed and looked at me with those disappointed eyes. It must be a requirement for teachers to know how to make you feel guilty just by looking at you.

"I really did!" I said, wanting desperately to be believed. "Look! I just grabbed the wrong book. I'll go get it."

"No, Sean. You know you can't go back to your locker. Bring it to me first thing after school."

"I will," I answered. She turned to begin class. "Mrs. Walker?" She turned back. "I really did finish it."

She smiled sadly and started the day's lesson.

Word had gotten around about my community service by lunchtime, in a big way. It gave me the opportunity to lay back and be cool for the afternoon. I didn't have to say anything; everybody else was telling my story for me. By the end of the day, the whole school "knew" that I was just kickin' at an old fart's ranch. They believed he was such an old geezer that I really didn't have to do any work, because he didn't pay attention to what got done.

But as soon as the last bell rang, I bolted. I've never moved so quickly through the hallways. I was in and out of my locker in record time. Mrs. Walker must have left early, so I left my paper on her desk on my way out.

I didn't even want to wait for the bus, so I jogged to the ranch. By the time I got there, I had a huge side cramp, and I was shaking all over. I wasn't in great shape. I mean, they make us take PE and all, but I hardly ever did anything in gym class, except maybe screw around. Having fifteen stitches in my shoulder didn't help either.

Gasping, I flopped down on the couch. I had tried to jog the whole way, but I had ended up doing a combination of jog and fast walk. I had to start getting in shape. It took me almost twenty minutes to do those two miles. The puppy came up and pounced on my shoelaces.

"Hey, pup," I panted. "I'll take you for a walk a little later, okay?"

"Where're your books?"

I looked up into Mr. H.'s frowning face. "Didn't need any. No homework tonight."

He didn't bat an eye, didn't say a word, just pointed at the door.

"What?"

"Go get your books."

"You're joking." But I knew he wasn't. "All right, I've got some math. But I can do that in study hall."

He just pointed to the door again.

"I can't. I can't run like that again. It would take me at least thirty minutes to get back, probably closer to forty-five."

I knew Mr. H. didn't care how long it would take for me to get my books. What mattered was me being able to do homework after dinner.

I argued halfheartedly for another couple minutes, even though I knew he wasn't going to change his mind. When I could tell he was getting really irritated with me, I started back toward the school.

Leaving the house, I couldn't make up my mind how I should go back to school. Should I take my time and prove a point to Mr. H.? Or should I hurry to get back to feed Knicker?

I walked as fast as I could.

The school looked as deserted as a tomb. Everyone was gone but the secretary and a couple of teachers. I was able to get to my locker. Not only did I have math, I also had a short story to finish for English, and a social studies worksheet. And I had forgotten to turn in my journal entries. Maybe it was worth going back for my books. I stopped to drop off my journal and to see if Mrs. Walker had picked up my paper. I guess she really had left school early, because the paper was still there, on top of the late paper basket.

When I stepped out of the school, snow had started to fall. I settled into a nice pace, enjoying the quiet flakes that drifted in circles on their way to the ground. I thought of Christmas, and for the first time in my life, I wondered where I would be then and what it would be like. I knew it wouldn't be like it had been the last five years. I wouldn't let it be.

I was a block and a half from the school when I got the feeling someone was behind me. I turned around, and my instincts proved to be right.

Rick was about ten feet back, and closing fast. He stopped abruptly when I turned around, but then continued with an even more arrogant strut.

"Yo, Farm Boy, I need a word with you."

"There's no farm boy for you to have a word with."

"Hey man, that's cool," he said, holding both hands out from his side. "You don't want to be called Farm Boy. Do me a small favor, and I'll see to it no one ever calls you Farm Boy again."

"No deal," I said, turning to continue on my way.

"Hey, man," he said, grabbing my jacket and spinning me around. "That ain't friendly. I ain't even asked you yet. How come you turn me down?"

"Nothing personal," I said, although we both knew it was, and I calmly removed his hand from my jacket. "I just don't believe in favors."

He stepped in close to my face, so close our noses almost touched. "Look, man," he growled, "I am really getting sick of you and your attitude. Somebody needs to straighten you out."

121

My stomach was doing back flips, the way it always did when I sensed a fight or action coming on, but I stayed ice-cold on the outside. "Well, you've been saying that for years. You finally gonna volunteer?" I drawled softly. "No, I don't think so. That would take...guts."

Rick took a slight step back and pulled his arm back, but he stopped at the honk of a horn. I glanced and saw a familiar beat-up blue truck pull up.

"Hey, Sean," James said, rolling down the window, "want a lift home?"

"Yeah," I said, "that'd be great."

"See ya later," Rick said, strutting off, "Farm Boy."

"Didn't mean to cut in on your conversation with your friend," James said as I got in.

"He's not my friend," I said shortly.

"Oh." James paused. "Well, that makes me feel better."

I glanced at him. "Why?"

"Well," he said, "you're not supposed to know this, but Boss sent me to give you a lift home. He felt bad about making you go back to school. Of course, I'm just supposed to be on my way home from the feed store, and I just happened to see you and offer you a ride."

I smiled. "I won't tell."

"Good." He nodded. "If I had thought you were just wasting time with a friend, I probably would have left you here. But, no offense, you two didn't look friendly."

"Like I said, we're not."

"You know, Sean, it'd be a real shame if you were to get in trouble so soon again. Especially if you really want to stay with Mr. H. The court wouldn't look on new trouble as a good reason for letting you stay."

"I know," I said, keeping my voice steady, even though I was seething inside. James didn't even know what had been going on, but right away he was directing the blame toward me.

I didn't say anything the rest of the drive home. I just sat and let the familiar anger eat at my mind.

As we got out, he turned to me with a grin. "That pup's been following the Boss around all day. I even caught him picking it up once or twice. I think between the two of you, you can convince him to keep it."

And just like that, my anger toward James melted away.

chapter sixteen

I dropped my books on the desk in my room and grabbed an apple off the kitchen table on my way to the stable. James said he thought Mr. H. was out there. That made it convenient for me. Everyone I wanted to see was in the same building.

I stopped at Knicker's stall first. He was almost bouncing off the walls. "Hey, boy, you want to go outside?" He head-butted my arm and I lost the apple. He beat me to it, slobbering on it and trying to eat it. He dropped it several times, but managed to get some small pieces off it before I got it back. When I took it from him, I kind of panicked. Were apples bad for horses? He didn't seem to think so. He was still trying to get at it.

Something tugged on my pant leg, and I looked down to see the puppy snarling at me, with my jeans firmly between his teeth. I looked up, and sure enough, Mr. H. was right behind him.

"How was your first day back?"

"Fine." I shrugged. "Except for having to walk there twice the first day."

It may have been my imagination, but I could have sworn he flushed just the slightest bit.

Knicker butted his head against my back, reminding me of my question. "Are apples bad for horses?"

He laughed. "Far from it. It's kind of like giving a special cut of steak to a dog. Why? Have you introduced Knicker to apples?"

"Accidentally." I told him about my lost apple.

"Well, it's good that he's interested enough in solid foods to go for the apple. He probably didn't get too much of it with his new teeth."

The puppy found a way to squirm in under the stall door. He and Knicker were both pretty interested in each other. Knicker blew on him and he scampered away, but then he yipped at Knicker, and it was Knicker's turn to jump.

Mr. H. cleared his throat. "The pup does seem to fit in here pretty well. He's not afraid of the horses and cattle, and he shows enough sense to stay out from under their feet. Maybe we ought to think of a good name for him."

I tried not to grin too broadly. "Well, I think that's your job."

"My job?"

"He is your puppy," I said, nodding toward the pup. He had come back out of the stall and was sitting patiently at Mr. H.'s feet. He never took his eyes off him, and his tail was cutting a wedge in the dirt from all the wagging.

Mr. Hassler leaned back against a stall, looking at the pup. "He reminds me of a dog that used to live up the road when I was a boy." He shook his head. "That was one slick dog. Prettiest thing you ever did see, and quite possibly the smartest. You know who Lassie is?"

"Sure, I've seen the reruns."

"Reruns, hah!" He shook his head. "Anyway, that dog could make Lassie look like a chump. Only he wasn't working from a script like Lassie did."

"So what was this wonder dog's name?"

He didn't answer, just watched the puppy for a few minutes. I was looking at the puppy, too, when Mr. H. softly said, "Cody."

The puppy stood up and whined, with his head cocked to one side, and increased his tail wagging. Now his whole body was twisting from one side to the other.

We looked at each other, not saying anything. Suddenly, Knicker stuck his nose over the half-door and nickered at us. We both burst out laughing.

"I might be wrong," he said, after we had calmed down a bit, "but I believe the name has been approved."

"I guess both names were," I agreed.

"C'mon, Sean. Let's go feed this little guy."

"And ourselves—I'm starving!"

"Hey, Cody, want to go out?" I asked. I was sitting at the kitchen table, doing makeup work. I had been there for the last hour and a half, and my brain was tired and my butt was sore. It was time to take a break.

Cody was curled up in his basket next to the oven, sleeping soundly. He didn't need to go out, but I did.

"Hey, Cody," I said, a little bit louder.

He looked up and blinked his eyes at me. He yawned, stretched his front legs straight out in front of him, and closed his eyes.

"Stupid dog, what good are you?" I asked crossly. I slumped down in the chair and hung my head over the back. I stopped when I saw Mr. H. upside down in the doorway.

"Hey," I said, straightening up.

"Hey, yourself. You look like you need to go play in the hay and wake up."

"I know. I was trying to get Cody to wake up so I would have a reason to go out."

Mr. H. just raised his eyebrows. I looked down at my feet.

There was Cody, sitting on my shoelace, looking wide awake.

"Stupid dog," I said again.

"Go on," Mr. Hassler said, "take him and take your fifteen-minute break."

The snow was still falling; it was already about three inches deep on the ground. I grabbed my jacket on the way out the back door and led Cody back behind the house to do his business. As little as he was, it didn't take long, so I thought we'd have time to wander down to the barn. I didn't hurry because Cody was having a great time in the snow, bouncing around and chasing snowflakes.

The minute I hit the light switch just inside the door, I knew something was wrong. I didn't know just what it was, but I felt my stomach tighten up.

I walked slowly down the row of stalls, trying to figure out what was wrong. A couple of the horses were dozing, but almost all of them were very awake—they seemed restless.

Knicker was backed into a far corner of his stall, and his eyes looked bigger than normal. I noticed he was shaking. He stayed in the corner even when I got close to his stall door. "Hey, Knick," I said softly, "what's up?"

I jumped back with my heart in my throat as a shadowy figure rose up from the nearest stall wall, right in front of my face. I was so busy looking down the barrel of a gun that it took me several seconds to focus my eyes on Rick.

"Bang," he said softly as he slowly lowered the hammer.

"What are you doing here?" I demanded.

"I asked you nicely to do me a favor, but you weren't very friendly."

"Rick, you and I both know you wouldn't do any favors for me. I don't need to do any for you. So why don't you just take off?"

"Oh, I'm so hurt," Rick whined sarcastically. "I'd do anything for you, Farmy."

I swallowed. *He actually has a gun,* I thought. *You'd better be careful.* "What do you want?"

"Oh, nothing. I'm just here to say hi."

The way he dragged out the last word and kind of almost sang it, I knew he was on something.

"Well, hi, Rick. Why don't you get out of here?"

"I will, Farm Boy, I will. But first we need to figure out a good time for me to come back on Wednesday."

"There isn't a good time on Wednesday. Just leave. We can say hi in the hallway."

He shook his head slowly, waving the pistol back and forth in front of my face. His eyes looked glazed, like he couldn't see straight. "No is not the right answer, Farm Boy. The deed is done. No one needs to get upset. Just tell me a good time to come back. And," he continued, stopping the pistol when it was aimed straight at Knicker's head, "I think you need to be a little more polite when you say it." He slowly pulled the hammer back.

I opened the stall door. Rick stared at me as I glanced around the stall. Knicker came over and stuck his head under my arm.

"Awww, ain't that cute. You've got you a overgrown mutt. He looks just like you, Farm Boy."

I saw what I had been looking for. While I was at school, I had heard about Rick's recent purchase. I was sure he was here looking for a hiding place, and he seemed to think Knicker's stall was the perfect spot. The straw was piled up in a corner, and I could see part of a plastic bag sticking out from the bottom of it.

"Rick, you're just going to have to find another place for your stash. It's no good here."

"Sure it is. No one's going to suspect some old farmer."

I shook my head. I was still trying to reason with him. If he hadn't had the pistol, I would have beat the tar out of him and that would have been the end of it. The gun changed all of the odds.

"No, Rick, it's not good. The horses not only kick the straw around and sleep on it, they also eat it. If you leave it in here, you've just spent a ton of money getting some horses really messed up."

He looked at me, and I could tell he was concentrating as hard as he could. Without drugs in his system he wasn't a bright thinker, but once he got high, almost all functions came to a stop.

"Now, see, you've pissed me off. You've wasted my time."

"How have I wasted your time?" I demanded.

"If you had been a little more cooperative this afternoon, this whole problem wouldn't exist. I wouldn't have wasted my time bringing all of this stuff out here. But since you weren't nice, you created a problem. So now." He leveled the gun at me. "Solve it, smart boy."

I had trouble following Rick's logic in how this was my problem, but I wasn't in any position to argue.

"Okay, give me details, and I'll see what I can do to help you out."

I think I might have eventually been able to talk Rick into leaving with his drugs. Another ten minutes and I might have been able to avoid the whole situation. Unfortunately, the timing was bad.

"Sean?" Mr. H. called down the row of stalls. Rick quickly dropped down behind the stall wall where he couldn't be seen. "Sean, your fifteen minutes are up."

"Be there in a minute," I responded, hoping my voice didn't reveal my fear. The pistol was aimed in my general direction, swaying ever so slightly.

"No, you'll be there *now.*" I could tell by his voice that he was getting closer.

"Get him out of here," Rick hissed at me. "Get him out of here, or…or… or I'll shoot your pony." When he aimed straight at Knicker's eye, the gun wasn't swaying anymore.

"Mr. H.," I called, trying desperately to think of something, anything that would possibly get him to leave. "I, uh, I'm just trying to find Cody. He wandered off."

I leaned over the stall door. My heart dropped to my stomach. Mr. Hassler was ten feet away. Cody was at his heels.

"I know," he said. "This pup learns quicker than you do. Fifteen minutes. We had a deal."

"I know, I know. I promise, I'll be right in. Just, um, just give me a few more minutes to say good night to Knicker."

"Knicker doesn't need you to tuck him in. What he does need is to have

127

you keep your butt out of trouble so you can be around to help him this winter. He's depending on you."

I risked a quick glance at Rick. He was still sitting with his back against the wall, and the gun was still trained on Knicker's head. Mr. H. had no idea how right he was.

Mr. Hassler looked like he was almost ready to come in the stall and get me.

"Mr. H., please! I just need a little more time to think."

"About what?"

I tried not to panic. "We read this story for English," I lied, "about this kid and his grandfather. And it got me thinking."

"What about it?"

"Well, it's really hard for me to talk about. Actually," I said, as Knicker moved away from me and stuck his nose over the door, "it's hard for me to think about. That's why I'd really like to have some more time by myself to think."

"Why?"

"Well, because it really reminded me of you."

He looked at me. He wasn't buying it. As frustrated as I was with Rick's stupidity, I was wishing Mr. H. would get a bad case of it right now. He was being too smart for his own good.

"See," I was grasping desperately at any straw I could find, "in this story, the guy was in World War II, and he had a run-in with an enemy soldier, and, well, it made me think of your story the other night, when you said that I wouldn't understand why the bullet was the most important thing, and you know, you were right, so I'm trying to figure it out right now but if I can't I'd like to talk to you about it later when I come back to the house." I was rambling and I knew it, but I couldn't stop.

Mr. H. was looking at me like he'd never seen me before. "Did you hit your head again?"

I shook my head.

"Do you think I hit *my* head?"

I shook my head again.

"Then why are you giving me this load of crap?"

"It's not a load of crap! Please, Mr. H., just give me ten more minutes. I swear, I'll be back in ten minutes!"

He looked at me. "You're a smart boy, Sean, and I think you know better than to pull this crap with me. I know you understand why the bullet's important to me."

"No, I don't, I really don't."

"I know you do, because you thanked me for the chocolate in the hospital."

"Yeah, yeah." The sweat was dripping down my back. "I thanked you because it's important, but I don't know why it's important." I could feel Rick's mocking stare pinning me to the wall. He was looking at me, but the gun was still trained on Knicker.

"I'll tell you why." His voice dropped and I could tell he was really angry with me. I really wanted to explain the whole thing to him. Tomorrow, when this was all over.

"The chocolate's important because it was the only thing he had left that seemed valuable to him. But the bullet's even more important, because it was absolutely the last thing he had to give, the last thing that he could use to defend himself and keep me at a distance, and he still gave it to me."

I looked at him, trying to plead with my eyes the way Knicker had that first day. "Can I please have some more time to think about that? So I can really understand it?"

"Well, now, Sean, I don't get what's going on here, but you can have all the time you need to think. At the kitchen table." His voice got hard. "Get your tail back up to the house where it belongs."

"But Mr. H.," I said desperately.

"Dammit, boy, can't you hold a bargain for even three days?" he bellowed, throwing open the stall door and barging in to get me.

He froze at the same gun report that made Knicker and me jump. Knicker bolted back to the far corner of his stall, while Mr. H. and I looked at Rick. He was lowering the pistol from over his head. *No one is hurt*, I thought. *He must have shot straight up.*

"I hate to break up this touching scene," he said sarcastically. "But it's making me sick. Sorry you had to be so persistent, Pops. I don't think you're going to agree to the favor I've been trying to talk Sean into." He leveled the gun at Mr. H. "So I think you may have to leave us soon."

"Rick, no!" I cried. "You can't. Without him, there's no ranch. You try to get rid of him and this place will be crawling with cops. Look, you've lost your hiding place. Just take off. I'll help you figure something else out tomorrow. We won't say anything."

"Like hell we won't," Mr. H. growled. I tried to get him to shut up, but he wouldn't listen. This was a man who had fought in one of the most horrible wars this planet had ever seen. This was a man who had pulled himself out of a hole when he was sixteen and never looked back. This was a man who had met life head-on and called his own shots. "How dare you try to push us around on my ranch?"

"It's easy," Rick said with a sick smile. "I dare because I have the gun."

"Rick," I said quickly, "this is between you and me. Put the gun down and we can ditch this guy. I'll help you out."

Rick slowly shook his head. "I don't think so. He got to you, man. You care about him. You're not ice-cold anymore. In fact, you're pretty useless."

I laughed, a short bark of a laugh. "I can't believe you actually thought I liked working here. I guess I ought to be an actor. I knew *he* had bought my snow job," I said, jerking my thumb toward Mr. H., "but I didn't think anyone else would."

"Nice try, Sean, but no good. This ain't no snow job."

"Get off my land!" Mr. H. suddenly exploded.

Rick sighed and looked at him. "You know, old man, you're a real pain. I think you've hung around too long." He started to raise the gun.

"It's over, Rick," I said quietly.

He looked at me in surprise, trying to hold the gun steady.

"It's over. This whole thing is stupid. Just put the gun down and walk away."

We stared at each other in silence. The horses in the other stalls had calmed down. Mr. H. and Knicker were forgotten. In his stare, I could feel all the hatred of the past years. *He's jealous*, I thought. *He knows I've found something important here.*

Suddenly he pulled the hammer back again. "Hmmm, now which one goes first?" he asked with a serious expression on his face.

"What do you mean?" I asked. My lips felt cold and dry.

"Well, Farm Boy, I warned you that if you didn't get rid of the old guy, I would have to kill your pony. So now they both have to go."

He won't do it, I said to myself. *He hasn't got the nerve.* "Rick," I tried again.

He began to shift his aim from Mr. H. to Knicker and back again, passing over me each time. "Eeennie, meeennnnie, mmmiiinnnieee..." He dragged out the last word, making his choice.

I can't take the chance, I thought. *I can't let him hurt Mr. H. or Knicker.*

Rick moved the gun back and forth, a wild look in his eyes. The instant I saw the gun move past Mr. H., I lunged at Rick.

I hit him, but I never felt it. The shot was loud, but it sounded strangely far away. I wanted to take the gun from him, but I couldn't get my hands up. My arms were numb. My chest was on fire. I tried to shake my head to stop the ringing in my ears, but I couldn't move at all.

Through a thick fog, I saw Mr. Hassler yank the gun from Rick's hand and then backhand him across the face with it. In slow motion he moved to my side. I saw his lips move, but the roar in my ears was so loud I couldn't hear him. I had to tell Mr. Hassler something. Something important.

Then everything went dark, and the last thing I felt was Knicker's warm breath on the back of my neck.

epilogue

Mrs. Walker came into Sean's hospital room. It was the third time she had been there in as many days. Mr. Hassler was in his usual post at the side of Sean's bed.

"You just missed his dad," Mr. Hassler said without looking up.

Mrs. Walker stood by the bed for a moment. She gently brushed the hair off Sean's forehead. Then she went over to Mr. Hassler.

"How is he?" she whispered.

"He's hanging in there. He came around for a few minutes earlier this morning. The doctors are hopeful."

Mrs. Walker reached over and squeezed Mr. Hassler's hand. "He's a tough kid."

"He'll make it," he finished for her.

They sat quietly for a few moments watching Sean breathe and listening to the various machines beep and hum.

"Oh," Mrs. Walker said. She reached into her bag and pulled out some papers. "Here. This is the essay Sean wrote about heroes. I thought you'd like to read it."

"Thank you, Michelle."

Mr. Hassler began to read.

My Hero is...

by Sean Parker

My hero is...no one. Heroes don't exist anymore, at least not in my world. Heroes used to come in all shapes and sizes, and that's why it's so sad that we XXX don't have them any more.

Our world today has taken the ancient "eye for an eye" motto

to the extreme of "whole estate for an eye." People are so caught
up with getting more, and having the best of all the more that they
can get, that they don't care how many toes, shoulders, or heads
that they step on to get there.

My hero is...no one.

Heroes used to exist in America. They've only recently disap-
peared. XXXXXXXX In fact, some people still try to be heroes. These
people are brave, loyal, morally XX right, and willing to sacrifice
themselves to help others. You've probably met such a hero.
Chances are good that when you met this hero, you recognized the
above qualities, but gave the hero a different name, like "chump,"
"suck-up," or "pathetic fool. XX"Somewhere along the line, people
quit respecting heroes. They're no longer looked up to, or even
supported. Look at Batman and Robin. The faithful readers of the
comic strip replied overwhelmingly to a poll the artist had. The
question was: "Should Robin live?" The nearly unanimous answer:
"No." They voted to kill a hero. It was a conscious decision re-
flecting an unconscious nation-wide trend.

Heroes used to stop along the roadside, just to help a stranded
soul change his tire. Today, that action may put your life in
danger, because you no longer know who has a gun in the glove box:
Is it the Hispanic in the XXXX El Camino, or the forty-year old
white business lady in the Probe? I don't know. Neither do the rest
of us. And we're not ready to take the chance of self-sacrifice to
find out.

My hero is...no one.

America had many war heroes. Men who kept going back into
battle, even after their fourth Purple Heart. Men who went back,
against orders, to save another man in their platoon. Men who went
into battle against incredible odds, knowing they might not
return home, but they went anyway, ready to sacrifice themselves
so that others might have the chance to have a better life.

Today, we don't fight many wars. Today, the people that most
school-age kids look up to are found XXXXXX in some sort of profes-

sional sport. Today, these men will quit a team they've been with for years, just to get an extra million for the season. Never mind the coach who saw their potential and developed it. Never mind the teammates who helped make them look good. Never mind the thousands of loyal fans who cheered whenever they saw them on the street. Never mind that they've already got twelve million socked away from the last three years. They want to get more. Why should they be loyal and sacrifice themselves to play a game they love for a team that supported them, if the other team will now offer four million instead of only three million? How on earth can we expect them to make such an incredible sacrifice?

My hero is...no one.

To name someone as your hero puts pressure on them. People don't want that XXXXX pressure. They don't want to be good or looked up to, because then they run the risk of failure. It's easier in this life to glide by. It's easier not to put yourself on the line by doing things for others.

My hero is...no one.

To name someone as your hero also makes you vulnerable. When your heroes fail, when they show themselves to be only human, it hurts. To name someone as your hero is to put your trust in them. And, as we all know, trusting someone other than yourself is risking being sacrificed.

Heroes still exist. They are no longer named, no longer recognized, no longer trusted. There are fewer and fewer heroes each year. I'm surprised they haven't been put on the endangered species list. If you find someone who is brave, loyal, and willing to do those extra things for you, don't say anything to him. Just stay close to him, and pay attention. You could learn a lot.

My hero is..XXX somewhere, I hope.